Valperga

Or, The Life And Adventures of Castruccio, Prince of Lucca
Vol. III

by

Mary Wollstonecraft Shelley

Valperga
Or, The Life And Adventures of Castruccio, Prince of Lucca
Vol. III
by Mary Wollstonecraft Shelley

ISBN: 978-93-67142-15-8

Published by

DOUBLE 9 BOOKS
2/13-B, Ansari Road
Daryaganj, New Delhi – 110002
info@double9books.com
www.double9books.com
Tel. 011-40042856

This book is under public domain

ABOUT THE AUTHOR

Mary Wollstonecraft Shelley was an English novelist best known for her groundbreaking work, "Frankenstein; or, The Modern Prometheus." Born in 1797, she was the daughter of feminist writer Mary Wollstonecraft and political philosopher William Godwin. Shelley's literary career began in the early 19th century, and she became a prominent figure in the Romantic literary movement.

Her works often explore themes of creation, ambition, and the human condition, reflecting her interest in science and ethics. In addition to "Frankenstein," she wrote several other novels, including "The Last Man" and "Valperga; or, The Life and Adventures of Castruccio, Prince of Lucca." Shelley's writing is characterized by its deep psychological insight and complex characters, particularly her portrayals of women navigating patriarchal societies. Shelley's influence extends beyond her lifetime, as her ideas and themes resonate in contemporary literature and discussions about gender, power, and morality. She remains a significant figure in both Gothic and science fiction literature.

CONTENTS

CHAPTER I

When Bindo had been released by the command of Castiglione from the hands of the Lucchese soldiers, he fled across the country; and, possessed with horror and despair at the issue of all his predictions, hastened to the only human being to whom he ever spoke his real sentiments, or in whom he placed any confidence.

To the north of Lucca, where the mountains rise highest, and the country is most wild, there was, at the period those people lived concerning whom I write, an immense ilex wood, which covered the Apennines, and was lost to sight in the grey distance, and among the folds and declivities of the hills. In this forest there lived a witch; she inhabited a cottage built partly of the trunks of trees, partly of stones, and partly was inclosed by the side of the mountain against which it leaned. This hut was very old; that part of it which was built of stone was covered with moss, lichens and wall-flowers, whose beauty and scent appeared alien to the gloom around; but, amidst desolation and horror, Nature loves to place the lovely and excellent, that man, viewing the scene, may not forget that she, the Mother, dwells every where. The trees were covered with ivy, many of them hollow and decaying, while around them the new sprouts arose, and refreshed the eye with an appearance of youth. On a stone near the cabin door sat the witch; she was very old; none knew how old: men, verging on decrepitude, remembered their childish fears of her; and they all agreed that formerly she appeared more aged and decrepid than now. She was bent nearly double; there was no flesh on her bones; and the brown and wrinkled skin hung loosely about her cheeks and arms. She was short, thin and small; her hair was perfectly white, and her red eyes, the only part about her that appeared to have life, glared within their sunken sockets; her voice was cracked and shrill.

"Well, son," said she, when she saw Bindo arrive, "What news? Are thine, or my predictions most true?"

Bindo threw himself on the ground, and tore his hair with rage, but he answered not a word.

"You would not believe my words," continued she, with a malicious laugh; "but the stars are not truer to their course, than I to fate; tomorrow not one stone will lie upon another of the castle of Valperga."

"This must not be," cried Bindo, starting up furiously; "it shall not be! Are you not a witch? and if you have sold your soul to the devil, will he not obey your will?"

"I sold my soul to the devil!" she replied in a tone, which bordered on a scream; "I tell thee, thou wert happy, if thy soul were as certain to be saved as mine. I rule the spirits, and do not serve them; what can angels do more? But one thing I cannot do; I cannot impede the star of Castruccio: that must rise."

"Aye,—you are all alike;—you can lame cattle, strangle fowls, and milk cows; but, when power is wanted, you are as weak as this straw. Come, if you are a witch, act as one."

"What would you that I should do? I can cover the sky with clouds; I can conjure rain and thunder from the blue empyrean; the Serchio will obey me; the winds from the north and the south know my call; the mines of the earth are subject to me, I can call the dead from their graves, and command the spirits of air to obey me. The fortunes of men are known to me; but man himself is not to be ruled, unless he consent to obey. Castruccio is set above men; his star is highest in the sky, and the aspect of the vast heaven favours him; I can do nothing with him."

"Then farewel; and may the curses of hell cling to you, and blight you! I want no conjuror's tricks,—but man shall do for me what the devil cannot."

"Stay, son," cried the witch; "now you say right; now you are reasonable. Though the star of Castruccio be high, it will fall at last, burst and fall like a dead stick upon the ground. Be it for us to hasten this moment; man may help you, and be that your task; watch all that happens, and tell me all; let no act or word escape your notice; and something will happen which I may wind to my purpose. We have both vowed to pursue the prince of Lucca to the death. There are no means now; but some will arise, and we shall triumph. Keep in mind one thing; do not let your mistress depart. I know that she desires to go to Florence; she must remain at Lucca, until the destined time be fulfilled; be it your task to keep her."

"I do not like these slow measures," replied the Albinois sullenly; "and, methinks, his waxen image at the fire, or his heart stuck full of pins, might soon rid the earth of him; surely if curses might kill a man, he were dead; tell me in truth is he not a fiend? Is he not one of the spirits of the damned housed in flesh to torment us?"

"Seek not to enquire into the mysteries of our art. You tell your wishes; I direct their accomplishment;—obey—you can do no more. When death, the mower, is in the field, few plants are tough enough to turn the edge of his scythe: yet Castruccio is one of these few; and patience and prudence alone can effect his fall. Watch every thing; report all to me; and beware that the countess leaves not Lucca; our power is gone, when she goes."

Such was the scene that immediately followed the destruction of the castle of Valperga. Bindo had hitherto loved his mistress, with an affection whose energy had never been called into action; but he loved her, as the lioness in the desert loves her whelps, who day by day feeds them in peace, but, when aroused by the hunters, will defend them to the last drop of her blood. He loved her, as we all love, and know not how fervently, until events awake our love to the expression of its energy. He had seldom thought upon Castruccio; when he came frequently to Valperga, and he saw his mistress happy in his visits, then these visits also made the Albinois joyful; yet he sympathized too little in the course of daily life, to disapprove of him when he came no more: but, when he sought to injure the sole being whom Bindo loved and reverenced, then a hidden spring suddenly burst forth in the Albinois' mind; and hate, till then unknown, arose, and filled every conduit of his heart, and, mingling its gall with the waters of love, became the first feeling, the prime mover in his soul.

He had long associated with this witch. He felt his defects in bodily prowess; perhaps also he felt the weakness of his reason; and therefore he sought for powers of art, which might overcome strength, and powers of mind, which were denied to the majority of the human species. Bindo was a very favourable subject for the witch to act upon; she deceived him easily, and through his means spread far the fame of her incantations. What made these women pretend to powers they did not possess, incur the greatest perils for the sake of being believed to be what they were not, without any apparent advantage accruing to themselves from this belief? I believe we may find the answer in our own hearts: the love of power is inherent in human nature; and, in evil natures, to be feared is a kind of power. The witch of the Lucchese forest was much feared; and no one contributed to the spread of this feeling more than Bindo.

She had no interest to preserve Euthanasia, or to destroy Castruccio; but she must feign these feelings in order to preserve her power over the Albinois. She resolved however not to be drawn into any action which might attract the hatred of the prince; for she knew him indeed to be a man out of her sphere, a man who went to mass, and told his beads as the church directed him, and who would have no hesitation in consigning to what he would call, condign punishment, all such as dealt with evil spirits, infernal drugs, and diabolical craft.

Bindo saw nothing of the motives which actuated her; and he really believed that the star of Castruccio had the ascendant: so after the first ebullitions of despair were calmed, he waited, with the patience of cherished hate, for the events which the witch told him might in the course of time bring about the sequel he so much desired.

He had made calculations, and cast lots upon the fate of Valperga, whose results were contrary to the enunciations of the witch. These had proved false; and, when time had calmed his feelings, this disappointment itself made him cling more readily to the distant, but as he hoped, surer promises of the witch, and build upon her words the certain expectation of the overthrow of Castruccio, and the restoration of Valperga in more than its original splendour. He returned to Euthanasia, and watched by her sick chamber, as the savage mother of a wild brood tends upon her expiring young; the fear of losing her by this sickness, at once exasperated him against the man whom he believed to be the cause of the mischief, and by the mightiness of his fear filled him with that calm which is the consummation of wretchedness. He neither ate nor slept; his existence appeared a miracle. But his mistress recovered; and his exhausted frame was now as much shaken with joy, as before with grief; yet, pale, emaciated, trembling as it were on the edge of life, but still living, he survived all these changes.

The summer advanced; and still Euthanasia remained at Lucca. A number of slight circumstances caused this: her health was yet weak; and her pale cheek and beamless eye shewed that life hardly sat firm upon his throne within her frame; they were menaced with a peculiarly hot season, and it was scarcely judged right that she should expose herself to the excessive heat of a Florentine summer. Lauretta also, her cousin, promised to accompany her, if she would delay her journey until autumn; so she consented to remain, although in truth she felt Lucca to be to her as a narrow prison, and cherished the hope of finding healthful feelings, and some slight return of happiness, at Florence. Yet the joyless state which was now her portion, was one reason why she cared not to change; it bred within her an indolence of feeling, that loved to feed upon old cares, rather than upon new hopes. A sense of duty, rather than any other sentiment, made her wish to remove; she believed, that she owed it to herself to revive from the kind of moral death she had endured, and to begin as it were a fresh life with new expectations. But we are all such creatures of habit, that we cling rather to sorrows which have been our companions of old, than to a new-sprung race of pleasures, whose very names perhaps are unknown to us.

Euthanasia loved to sit in the desolate garden of her palace, and to moralize in her own mind, when she saw a tender rose embraced and choked by evil weeds that grew in strength about it; or sometimes to visit the tower of her palace, and to look towards the rock where the castle of Valperga had once stood, now a heap of ruins. Could she endure to look upon the formless mass which had before constituted her shelter and home? where had stood the hall within whose atmosphere she had grown to womanhood; where she had experienced all the joys that her imagination and heart (storehouses of countless treasure) could bestow? Yet that was all gone, and she must begin life anew: she prayed for her father's spirit to inspire her with courage; but her mind was too subtle and delicate in its feelings, to forget its antient attachments. There are some souls, bright and precious, which, like gold and silver, may be subdued by the fiery trial, and yield to new moulds; but there are others, pure and solid as the diamond, which may be shivered to pieces, yet in every fragment retain their indelible characteristics.

"I can never change," she thought, "never become other than I am. And yet I am told that this obstinate sorrow is weakness, and that the wise and good, like strong plants, shoot up with fresh vigour, when cut down even to the root. It may be so; and so it may perhaps be with me: but as yet I feel all dead, except pain, and that dwells for ever within me. Alas! life, and the little it contains, is not worth the misery I endure; its best joys are fleeting shadows; its griefs ought to be the same; and those are true philosophers, who trample on both, and seek in the grave for a wisdom and happiness, which life cannot bring us.

"Why was I born to feel sorrow? Why do I not die, that pain may expire with me? And yet I now speak as a presumptuous caviller, unread in the lessons of the wise, and who vainly blunders over and misquotes their best learning. Life has more in it than we think; it is all that we have, all that we know.

"Life is all our knowledge, and our highest praise is to have lived well. If we had never lived, we should know nothing of earth, or sky, or God, or man, or delight, or sorrow. When our Creator bestowed on us this gift, he gave us that which is beyond all words precious; for without it our apparent forms would have been a blind atom in the mass, our souls would never have been. We live; and we learn all that is good, and see all that is beautiful; our will is called into action, our minds expand like flowers, till, overworn, they fade; if we did not live, we should know nothing of all this; and if we do not live well, we reap sorrow alone.

"What do we know of heroes and sages, but that they lived? Let us not spurn therefore this sum and summit of our knowledge, but, cherishing it, make it so appear that we value, and in some degree deserve, the gift of life, and the many wonders that accompany it."

Euthanasia suffered much during the summer months; and all that she heard of Castruccio turned the fount of wholesome tears to drops of agony. He had in truth become a tyrant. He did not slay his thousands like Ezzelin of Padua; but he had received the graft of vain-glory into his soul, and he now bore the fruits. He put to death remorselessly those whom he suspected, and would even use torture, either to discover other victims, or to satisfy his desire of revenge. Several circumstances of this kind happened during this summer, which made Euthanasia more miserable than words or tears could express. If she saw his enemies, they uttered deep curses on his cruelty; if she saw those who had formerly been his friends, their talk was filled with bitter sarcasms on his ingratitude, and careless coldness of heart. That heart had once been the garden of virtue, where all good qualities sprung up and flourished, like odorous and delicately painted flowers; but now ambition had become its gardener, and the weed-overgrown inclosure of Euthanasia's palace was but a slight symbol of all of cruel and treacherous that sprung up there, which allowed no rose to blow, and hid the blooms of the jessamine in the coarse and broad leaves of worthless brambles. Sometimes she thanked Providence that she had not become the wife of this man: but it was a bitter thankfulness. She had not been wedded to him by the church's rites; but her soul, her thoughts, her fate, had been married to his; she tried to loosen the chain that bound them eternally together, and felt that the effort was fruitless: if he were evil, she must weep; if his light-hearted selfishness allowed no room for remorse in his own breast, humiliation and sorrow was doubly her portion, and this was her destiny for ever.

His military exploits of this year rather consisted in the slow laying of foundation-stones, than were distinguished by any peculiar glory. The Florentine army retreated in trepidation before him; he took several castles, made several new alliances, and consolidated more and more the power which he hoped one day to put to a mighty purpose. Desire of dominion and lordship was the only passion that now had much power in his soul; he had forgotten Euthanasia; or if he remembered her, he called her a peevish girl, and wasted no further thought upon her.

The summer had been tremendously hot; and all the fields were parched, and the earth baked and cracked from the long drouth. These were all signs of a wet autumn; and hardly had Euthanasia determined on her journey to Florence, before it was stopped by tremendous rains and tempests, that deluged the earth, and disturbed the sky. The lightning became as a shaft in the hands of an experienced warrior; so true it seemed to its aim, and destroying so many with its subtle fire: and the thunder, reverberating along the hills, sent up to heaven the shout, which proclaimed the triumph and desolation of its precursor. Then came the rain; and the earth gladly received these tokens of heaven's love, which blessed her with fertility. The torrents roared down the hills; and the rivers, no longer restrained within their banks, rose, and deluged the plain, filling even the streets of Lucca with water.

Bindo looked on all this labour of the elements with a mind hovering between pleasure and fear. He believed that the witch of the forest had caused this inundation, to impede the journey of the countess; but, thinking thus, he trembled at the power she possessed, and at the strange company of unseen spirits, which thus, unknown to mortals, interfere with their destinies. The devil, he knew, was called prince of the air; but there is a wide difference between our belief of an hearsay, and the *proof* which he now thought was presented to him. When he repaired at the mysterious hour of midnight to a running stream, and saw, as the witch uttered her incantations, and lashed the waters with her rod,—that a tempestuous wind arose from the south, and the dark clouds among which the lightnings played, advanced over their heads, and then the rain in quick big drops, accompanied by hail, fell on the earth;—when he saw this, his limbs trembled, his heart beat quick with fear; he dared not cross himself, nor mutter a *pater-noster*; and, if love and hate had not possessed him so entirely, he would never have ventured again to witness the magical powers of his friend.

A cold and early winter followed the flood, and froze the waters before they retreated from the inundated fields. For many years so terrible a season had not been known in Italy and, in the Lucchese states particularly, it occasioned a great loss of fruit-trees and vines. The mountains were covered with snow; the torrents were arrested in their course by the subtle nets which winter cast over them; it was a strange sight for an Italian to see. "And this," thought Euthanasia, "is what the Trans-alpines mean, when they talk of the fearful cold of winter. Oh! indeed, no hunter is like him, when he comes down from the north, bringing frost, his bride, along with him; he hunts the leaves from the trees, and destroys the animals which inhabit the earth, even in their holds and fastnesses. He casts bonds upon the rivers and streams; and even the 'sapless foliage of the ocean,' and the mighty monsters and numberless spawn that rove through its wastes, are all subdued by his fierce and resistless ravages."

Thus she thought, as she saw the country late so beautiful, the Earth, lovely as a young mother nursing her only care, now as wild and forlorn as that mother if she be ruthlessly bereft of her infant. The fields were hardened by frost; and the flood lay moveless and white over the plain; the hills were covered with snow. It was a grievous change from the smiles of summer; but it did not last long; and thaw quickly reversed the scene. The earth was again alive; and the rivers and floods again filled the air with sound. Euthanasia resolved to wait only until the season should be somewhat more advanced, to make her long delayed journey to Florence.

CHAPTER II

While Euthanasia yet remained at Lucca in this uncertain manner, a circumstance occurred which caused her to suspend the preparations for her journey. Late one night (it was nearly twelve o'clock), the visit of a stranger was announced; a man, they said, so wrapt up in his capuchin, that his physiognomy could not be distinguished. Why did Euthanasia's heart beat fast, and the colour desert her warm lips? What could she hope or fear? The man was admitted, and one glance sufficed to satisfy her curiosity, and to quiet her trembling expectation. He was one of the meaner class; and, when he threw back his cloak, Euthanasia perceived that he was an entire stranger to her; but there was a kindness, a rough sensibility in his face, that pleased her, and she gently enquired what he had to say to her.

"Noble countess, I come on a work of charity, which would ruin me for ever if my superiors were to discover it. I am the jailor of the Lucchese prison; and this morning the Dominican inquisitors put under my custody a Paterin woman[1], whom it would move any soul but theirs to behold. She has touched me with the greatest pity by her tears and heart-breaking intreaties: she denies her heresy, and says that you can prove her faith; but she must see you first; and I, at peril of all that I am worth, am come to conduct you to her dungeon, for I can admit you only by night. Surely you will come; poor thing, she is very young and fearful, and is now lying on the floor of her prison panting with terror and expectation."

"Unfortunate creature! Did she tell you her name?"

"She says that you do not know it; but she intreats you to remember a pilgrim girl, whom you once received at your castle, and whom you pitied; a sun-burnt, way-worn creature who said that she was on the way to Rome."

"I do not recollect; but if she is unhappy, and desires to see me, it is enough, I follow you."

Euthanasia wrapt her capuchin around her, and followed the man through the dark, wet streets of Lucca: the thaw had not yet completed its work; the snow was deep and miry under their feet; while the melting collections of several days dripped, or rather streamed from the house-roofs on their heads: the Libeccio blew a warm, cloud-bringing wind, that made the night so black, that they could not avoid the standing pools that interspersed the streets. At length they arrived at the prison; the jailor entered by a small, low door which he carefully closed after them, and then struck a light. He led Euthanasia through the bare and mildewed vaults, sometimes unlocking a massy gate, drawing back the harsh bolts which grated with rust and damp; sometimes they emerged into a passage open to the sky, but narrow, with tall black walls about it, which dropt their melted snow with a continual and sullen splash upon the pavement: small, glassless, grated windows looked into these strait passages; these were the holes that admitted light into the dungeons. At length they ascended a small, broken, staircase of wood; and, opening a door at the head of it, and consigning his lamp to the countess, the jailor said: "She is here; comfort her; in two hours I shall come to conduct you back."

Euthanasia entered the prison-chamber, awe-stricken and trembling; for the good ever feel humiliated at the sight of misfortune in others: the poor prisoner was seated crouched in a corner; she looked wildly towards the door; and, seeing Euthanasia, she leaped up, and, throwing herself at her feet, clinging to her knees, and clasping them with convulsive strength, she cried, "Save me! You alone on earth can save me."

Poor Euthanasia was moved to tears; she raised the sufferer, and, taking her in her arms, tried to soothe her: the prisoner only sobbed, leaning her head upon Euthanasia's hand: "Fear not, you shall be saved; poor sufferer, calm yourself; speak, what would you with me? fear not, no harm shall reach you; I will be your friend."

"Will you indeed—indeed—be my friend? and go to him, and bid him save me? He alone can do it."

"Who? Speak calmly, dearest; pause awhile; reassure yourself, and then speak. Look, you are safe in my arms; I clasp them round you, do not fear!"

The prisoner sunk in Euthanasia's embrace: she was chilled, icy-cold;— and she lay panting, as a bleeding fawn who gazes on its death's wound. The warmth of Euthanasia's arms somewhat restored her; and she said, dividing the entangled strings of her hair with her thin fingers; "You do not remember me, nor would he; I am as unlike what I was when he saw me, as is the yellow, fallen leaf to the bright-green foliage of May. You do not remember me?"

"Yes, now it flashes on my memory; are you then indeed——" Euthanasia paused; the name of Beatrice hovered on her lips, but a feeling of delicacy prevented her from speaking it: she continued; "Yes, I recollect the pilgrim, your refusal to remain at Valperga, and the deep interest I took in your sorrows."

"You were very, very kind; are you not so now? Will you not go to him, and ask him to order my release?"

"To whom am I to go? and from whom do I come?" asked Euthanasia, half-smiling; for, notwithstanding the prisoner recalled to her memory a scene, which made it appear that she was certainly Beatrice; yet so long had all trace of her been lost, that she wished for some confirmation from her own lips.

"Alas!" replied the unhappy girl, "I would not have him know, if I could help it. Do you think that, if you were to tell him that a poor girl, who five years ago had just attained her seventeenth year, who was then happy, loving and adored,—who is now pursued for heresy—falsely—or if you will—truly; one very unfortunate, who earnestly implores him as he loves his own soul, to save her; do you not think he would compassionate me?"

"Who? you speak in riddles."

"In riddles! Are you not Euthanasia? You must know whom I mean; why, Antelminelli,—Castruccio."

The prisoner hid her face with her hands. She blushed deeply, and her fast-falling tears trickled through her fingers; Euthanasia blushed also, a tremulous hectic, that quickly vanished, while her companion's cheeks still burned.

"Yes, I will go to him, or to any one on earth to save you.—Yet methinks I had better go to the father-inquisitors; I am known to them, and I think I could as easily move them as the prince; he is careless——"

"Oh! no—no; you must go to him: he knew me once, and surely would compassionate me. Try him first with the echo of my complaints, and a relation of my tears; surely his eyes, which can look into the soul, would then be dimmed: would they not?"

Euthanasia thought of Leodino; and she was about to reply, that warriors, politicians, and ambitious princes, such as Castruccio, were accustomed to regard with contempt woes like hers. But she hesitated; she would not rob him, whom she had once loved, of the smallest mite of another's praise, however undeserved; besides, she felt that the name of Beatrice alone would move him to compassion, perhaps to remorse. She was therefore silent; and the prisoner continued, with a voice of trembling earnestness, "Try every argument first; but, if he is obdurate, then tell him that he once knew me,—that now my fortunes are changed,—he will guess the cause: yet perhaps he will think wrong, for *that* is not the cause. Tell him I am one Beatrice;—he saw me some years ago at the house of the good bishop of Ferrara."

The poor fallen prophetess now burst into a passion of weeping; she wrung her hands, and tore her hair, while her companion looked on her, unable to restrain her tears. Castruccio had described his Beatrice, so bright, so ethereal in her loveliness, that it moved Euthanasia's inmost soul to see what a change a very few years had made. Perceiving the blushes and shame of the lost girl, she concealed her knowledge of her tale, and answered only by endeavouring to soothe her, and to assure her of her safety.

"Am I safe? I tell you that I fear, oh! how much I fear! I am very young; I was once happy; but, since that, I have suffered beyond human utterance; yet I dread death; and, more than all, do I fear pain. They call me a heretic; aye," (and her dark eyes beamed fiercely) "I am one; I do not belong to their maudlin creed; I feel my wrongs, and I dare curse— —But, hush, not so loud.—You pardon me, do you not? Alas! if you turn against me, they seize on me, tear me, burn me!"

The two hours had swiftly passed, while Beatrice thus wept with alternate passion. The jailor came to reconduct Euthanasia; but Beatrice clung to her, clasping her neck, and intwining her fingers in her long thick hair. "No! no! You must not go!" she cried; "I shall die, if I am again left alone. Oh! before you came, I sometimes felt as if I did not know where I was, and madness seemed about to fall on me: you are good, consolatory, kind; you must not leave me."

"Then I cannot see the prince; I cannot intercede for your liberation."

"But that is many hours hence, and the comfortable day-light will be come; now it is quite dark; hark to the splashing water, and the howling of the Libeccio; I had forgotten all that; and now they come upon me with ten-fold horror; do not leave me!"

Euthanasia could hardly distinguish the suppliant's features by the light of the jailor's small lamp; but she saw her eyes bright with tears, and felt her bosom throb against her own; again she strove to console her; reason was thrown away;—when the jailor urged his, her own, every one's safety—she shook her head.

"I thought you were kind; but you are not: my cheeks are pale with fear; put up your lamp to them that you may see. She can go early, the moment day dawns,—indeed she shall go then, but now she must not."

Euthanasia tore herself away; though her heart was pierced by the wild shriek of Beatrice, as she threw herself on the floor. The jailor led her through the melancholy passages of the prison, and then along the wet streets, until she reached her home: and she retired to meditate during the remaining hours of night on the words she should employ in her representations to Castruccio the following morning.

The expectation of this meeting flushed her cheeks, and made her deep eyes beam, while every limb trembled. She had not seen him so long that his assumed power, his tyrannies, and mean politics, were lost in her recollection; she felt as if she should again see him honest, passion-breathing, and beautiful, as when they took sweet counsel together at Valperga. Valperga! that was now a black and hideous ruin, and he the author of its destruction. But she thought, "This is a dream;—I shall see him, and it will vanish; there is a coil wound round me of sorrow and distrust, which will snap beneath his smile, and free me,—I shall see him!

"Why do I think of myself? I go to free this poor girl, whom he has wronged, and to whom he belongs far more than to me; this unhappy Beatrice, who sheds tears of agony in her dungeon. I am nothing; I go as nothing; would that he should not recognize me! I go a suppliant for another, and I must tame my looks: they are not proud; but I must teach them humility; I must school my heart not to speak, not to think of itself—I go for her; and, having obtained my request, I will come away, forgetful that I am any thing."

Day dawned; day, cold, wet, and cloudy, but ever cheerful to one weighed down by the sense of darkness and inaction: day did not dawn this dreary winter morning, until seven o'clock, and the period had arrived when it was fitting that Euthanasia should seek Castruccio. She threw a veil over her shining hair, while she hid her form in a rich cloak of sables; then she stole out alone; for she could not endure that any one should know of this strange visit. When, she arrived at the *Palazzo del Governo*, her rich attire and distinguished mien won her easy entrance, and she penetrated to the cabinet of the prince.

Her heart beat audibly; she had entered with rapid, though light steps; now she paused; and, as it were gathering up the straggling feelings of her mind, she endeavoured to bind them in a firm knot; she resolved to calm herself, to still the convulsive motion of her lips, to remember nothing but Beatrice. She entered; Antelminelli was alone; he was at a table reading a paper, and a smile of light derision played upon his features; he raised on her his dark, piercing eyes, and seeing a lady before him, he rose; in a moment Euthanasia was self-possessed and resolved; and casting back her cloak, and throwing aside her veil, her eyes lifted up, yet not fixed on him, she began in her silver voice to say, "My lord, I come— —"

But he was too much thunderstruck to listen; his cheeks glowed with pleasure; all the anger and indifference he had nourished vanished in her presence, and he broke forth in a torrent of wonder and thanks.

She waved her hand,—"Do not thank me, but listen; for I come on a message, an errand of charity; and if you can, hear me, and forget who it is that speaks."

He smiled, and replied: "Certainly it were easy not to see the sun when it shines: but, whatever your errand may be, speak it not yet;—if you come to make a request, I shall grant it instantly, and then you will go; but pause awhile first, that I may look on you; it is a whole year since I saw you last; you are changed, you are paler,—your eyes—but you turn away from me, as if you were angry."

"I am not angry—but I am nothing.—There is a heretic, at least a girl accused of heresy, confined in your prisons, whom I wish you to free, and, for the love of Heaven, not by the shortest delay to add another moment of sorrow to her heap: she has suffered much."

"A heretic! that is beyond my jurisdiction; I do not meddle with religion."

"Yes, you do;—you see priests every day: but I intreat you not to oblige me to argue with you; listen to me a few moments, and I shall say no more. She is very unfortunate, and fears death and pain with a horror that almost deprives her of reason; she is young; and it is piteous to see one scarcely more than twenty years of age, under the fangs of these bloodhounds; she was once happy; alas! pity her, since she feels to the very centre of her heart the change from joy to grief."

"Yet no harm will happen to her, at most a few months' imprisonment: if she dread death and pain, she will of course recant and be freed; what will she suffer for so short a time?"

"Fear; the worst of evils, far worse than death. I would fain persuade you to throw aside this hard-heartedness, which is not natural to you; moments are years, if they are lengthened out by pain; every minute that she lives in her dungeon is to her a living death of agony; but I will tell you her name,—at her request I wished to conceal it: but that will win you, if you are not already won by the sweet hope of saving one who suffers torments you can never know."

"Euthanasia, do not look so gloomily; I am not thinking of your heretic; I hesitate, that I may keep you here: you have your will; I will never refuse a request of yours."

A smile of fleeting disdain passed over her countenance. "Nay, when you know who she is, you may grant my prayer for her own sake. I come from Beatrice, the daughter of Wilhelmina of Bohemia."

If the ghost of the poor prophetess had suddenly arisen, it could not have astounded Castruccio more, than to hear her name thus spoken by Euthanasia, coupled with the appellations of heretic and prisoner. The tide of his life ebbed; and, when it flowed again, he thought of the celestial Beatrice, her light step, her almost glorious presence; and the memory of her pale cheek and white lips when he last saw her, thrilled his heart. Years had passed since then; what had she suffered? What was she? A heretic? Alas! she was the daughter of Wilhelmina, the nursling of Magfreda, the ward of a leper, the adopted child of the good bishop of Ferrara.

Euthanasia saw the great confluence of passions, which agitated Castruccio, and made him alternately pale and red; she was silent, her quiet eyes beaming upon him in compassion; for a long time his heart could not find a voice, but at length he spoke, —"Hasten! hasten! free her, take her to you! Euthanasia, you are the angel itself of charity; you know all her sad story—all that relates to me; calm her, console her, make her herself again,—poor, poor Beatrice!"

"Farewell then; I go,—send one of your officers with the order; I will hasten to her, as quickly as you can wish."

"Yet pause, stay one moment; shall I never see you again? You have cast me off utterly; yet, I pray you, be happy. Why should you be pale and sorrowful? you have other friends; must all that love me, mourn? Surely I am not a devil, that all I touch must wither. Beware! tear the veil from your heart; read, read its inmost secrets, the eternal words imprinted in its core; you do not despise me, you love me,—be mine."

The pale cheek of Euthanasia was flushed, her eyes flashed fire,— "Never! tie myself to tyranny, to slavery, to war, to deceit, to hate? I tell thee I am as free as air. But I am hurried far beyond the bounds I prescribed for myself, and now not a word more."

"Yes, one word more; not of yourself, wild enthusiast, but of Beatrice. I destroyed her; not that I knew what I did; but heedlessly, foolishly, destroyed her; do you then repair my work; I would give half my soul that she should be as when I first saw her. You have heard a part of her story, and you will now perhaps learn those sufferings which she has endured since we parted; it is doubtless a strange and miserable tale; but do you be the ministering angel of mercy and love to her."

Sorrow and even humiliation were marked on Castruccio's countenance; Euthanasia looked at it, almost for the first time since she had entered; she sighed softly, and said nearly in a whisper, "Alas! that you should no longer be what you once were!"

Pride now returned and swelled every feature of Castruccio; "Enough, enough: whatever wine of life I drain, I mingled it myself. Euthanasia, if we never meet again, remember, I am content; can you be more?"

Euthanasia said not a word; she vanished, her bright presence was gone; and Castruccio, to whom, as to the fallen arch-angel, that line might be applied,

Vaunting aloud, though rack'd with deep despair,

tearless, his lips pressed together, sat recalling to mind her words and looks, until, remembering his boast, he looked up with angry defiance; and, shaking from his heart the dew of tenderness, he plunged amidst the crowd where he commanded, where his very eye was obeyed.

Euthanasia hastened to the prison, where the kind-hearted jailor led her with a face of joyful triumph to the dungeon of Beatrice; the poor thing was sleeping, the traces of tears were on her cheeks (for like a child she had cried herself to sleep), and several times she started uneasily. Euthanasia made a sign to the jailor to be silent, and knelt down beside her, looking at her countenance, once so gloriously beautiful; the exquisite carving of her well shaped eyelids, her oval face, and pointed chin still shewed signs of what she had been; the rest was lost. Her complexion was sun-burnt, her hands very thin and yellow, and care had already marked her sunken cheeks and brow with many lines; her jet black hair was mingled with grey; her long tresses had been cut, and now reached only to her neck; while, strait and thin, they were the shadow merely of what they had been; her face, her whole person was emaciated, worn and faded. She awoke and beheld the eyes of Euthanasia, like heaven itself, clear and deep, gazing on her.—"Arise, poor sufferer, you are free!"

Beatrice looked wildly; then, starting up, she clapped her hands in a transport of joy, she threw herself at the feet of her deliverer, she embraced the jailor, she was frantic. "Free! free!" for some time she could repeat no other word. At length she said, "Pardon me; yesterday I was rude and selfish; I tormented and reproached you, who are all kindness. And you, excellent man, you will forgive me, will you not? What was it that I feared? Now that I am going to leave my dungeon, methinks it is a good cell enough, and I could stay here always well content; it is somewhat dark and cold, but one can wrap oneself up, and shut one's eyes, and fancy one's self under the sun of heaven."

She continued prattling, and would have said much more, but that Euthanasia with gentle force drew her from the dungeon, out of the gloomy prison; and they hastened to her palace, where Beatrice was quickly refreshed by a bath and food. But, when the first joy of liberation was passed, she sunk to melancholy: she would not speak, but sat listlessly, and her tears fell in silence. Euthanasia tried to comfort her; but many days passed, during which she continued sullen and untractable.

In the mean time Euthanasia received several billets from Castruccio, with earnest enquiries concerning the welfare of this poor girl. "God knows," he wrote, "what has happened to this unfortunate being since we parted. My heart is agonized, not only for what she suffers, but for what she may have suffered. She is now, they say, a heretic, a Paterin, one who believes in the ascendancy of the evil spirit in the world; poor insane girl! Euthanasia, for her soul's sake, and for mine which must answer for hers, reason with her, and convert her; be to her as an affectionate sister, an angel of peace and pardon. I leave the guidance of her future destiny to your judgement: but do not lose sight of her. What do I ask of you? And what right have I to bring upon you the burthen of my faults? But you are good, and will forgive me."

> [1] These heretics were long a principal subject of hostility to the Inquisition; and in 1290 a particular community was erected at Florence by San Pietro di Verona, for the express purpose of their extermination.

CHAPTER III

Euthanasia was meditating on this letter, when Beatrice entered, and sat down beside her. She took her hand, and kissed it, and then said, "How can you forgive my ingratitude? I am self-willed, sullen, and humorous; alas! sometimes the memory of the evils I have suffered presses on me, and I forget all my duties. Duties! until I knew you I had none; for five years my life has been one scene of despair: you cannot tell what a fall mine was."

"Forget, I do intreat you, poor sufferer, all your past unhappiness; forget every thing that you once were."

"Aye, you say right; I must forget every thing, or to be what I am must torture me to despair. Poor, misled, foolish, insensate Beatrice! I can accuse myself alone for my many ills; myself, and that power who sits on high, and scatters evil like dew upon the earth, a killing, blighting honey dew."

"Hush! my poor girl, do not talk thus; indeed I must not have you utter these sentiments."

"Oh! let me speak: before all others I must hide my bursting feelings, deep, deep. Yet for one moment let me curse!"

Beatrice arose; she pointed to heaven; she stood in the same attitude, as when she had prophesied to the people of Ferrara under the portico of the church of St. Anna; but how changed! Her form thin; her face care-worn; her love-formed lips withered; her hands and arms, then so round and fair, now wrinkled and faded; her eyes were not the same; they had lost that softness which, mingling with their fire, was as something wonderful in brilliancy and beauty; they now, like the sun from beneath a thunder cloud, glared fiercely from under her dark and scattered hair that shaded her brow: but even now, as in those times, she spoke with tumultuous eloquence:

"Euthanasia, you are much deceived; you either worship a useless shadow, or a fiend in the clothing of a god. Listen to me, while I announce to you the eternal and victorious influence of evil, which circulates like air about us, clinging to our flesh like a poisonous garment, eating into us, and destroying us. Are you blind, that you see it not? Are you deaf, that you hear no groans? Are you insensible, that you feel no misery? Open your eyes, and you will behold all of which I speak, standing in hideous array before you. Look around. Is there not war, violation of treaties, and hard-hearted cruelty? Look at the societies of men; are not our fellow creatures tormented one by the other in an endless circle of pain? Some shut up in iron cages, starved and destroyed; cities float in blood, and the hopes of the husbandman are manured by his own mangled limbs: remember the times of our fathers, the extirpation of the Albigenses;—the cruelties of Ezzelin, when troops of the blind, and the lame, and the mutilated, the scum of his prisons, inundated the Italian states. Remember the destruction of the templars. Did you never glance in thought into the tower of famine of Ugolino; or into the hearts of the armies of exiles, that each day the warring citizens banish from their homes? Did you never reflect on the guilty policy of the Popes, those ministers of the reigning king of heaven? Remember the Sicilian vespers; the death of the innocent Conradin; the myriads whose bones are now bleached beneath the sun of Asia: they went in honour of His name, and thus He rewards them.

"Then reflect upon domestic life, on the strife, hatred and uncharitableness, that, as sharp spears, pierce one's bosom at every turn; think of jealousy, midnight murders, envy, want of faith, calumny, ingratitude, cruelty, and all which man in his daily sport inflicts upon man. Think upon disease, plague, famine, leprosy, fever, and all the aching pains our limbs suffer withal; visit in thought the hospital, the lazar house; Oh! surely God's hand is the chastening hand of a father, that thus torments his children! His children? his eternal enemies! look, I am one! He created the seeds of disease, maremma, thirst, want; he created man,—that most wretched of slaves; oh! know you not what a wretch man is? and what a store house of infinite pain is this much-vaunted human soul? Look into your own heart; or, if that be too peaceful, gaze on mine; I will tear it open for your inspection. There is remorse, hatred, grief—overwhelming, mighty, and eternal misery. God created me: am I the work of a beneficent being? Oh, what spirit mingled in my wretched frame love, hope, energy, confidence,—to find indifference, to be blasted to despair, to be as weak as the fallen leaf, to be betrayed by all! Now I am changed,—I hate;—my energy is spent in curses, and if I trust, it is to be the more deeply wounded.

"Did not the power you worship create the passions of man; his desires which outleap possibility, and bring ruin upon his head? Did he not implant the seeds of ambition, revenge and hate? Did he not create love, the tempter: he who keeps the key of that mansion whose motto must ever be

Lasciate ogni speranza voi che intrate.

And the imagination, that masterpiece of his malice; that spreads honey on the cup that you may drink poison; that strews roses over thorns, thorns sharp and big as spears; that semblance of beauty which beckons you to the desart; that apple of gold with the heart of ashes; that foul image, with the veil of excellence; that mist of the maremma, glowing with roseate hues beneath the sun, that creates it, and beautifies it, to destroy you; that diadem of nettles; that spear, broken in the heart! He, the damned and triumphant one, sat meditating many thousand years for the conclusion, the consummation, the final crown, the seal of all misery, which he might set on man's brain and heart to doom him to endless torment; and he created the Imagination. And then we are told the fault is ours; good and evil are sown in our hearts, and ours is the tillage, ours the harvest; and can this justify an omnipotent deity that he permits one particle of pain to subsist in his world? Oh, never.

"I tell thee what; there is not an atom of life in this all-peopled world that does not suffer pain; we destroy animals;—look at your own dress, which a myriad of living creatures wove and then died; those sables,—a thousand hearts once beat beneath those skins, quenched in the agonies of death to furnish forth that cloak. Yet why not? While they lived, those miserable hearts beat under the influence of fear, cold and famine. Oh! better to die, than to suffer! The whale in the great ocean destroys nations of fish, but thousands live on him and torment him. Destruction is the watchword of the world; the death by which it lives, the despair by which it hopes: oh, surely a good being created all this!

"Let me tell you, that you do ill to ally yourself to the triumphant spirit of evil, leaving the worship of the good, who is fallen and depressed, yet who still lives. He wanders about the world a proscribed and helpless thing, hooted from the palaces of kings, excommunicated from churches; sometimes he wanders into the heart of man, and makes his bosom glow with love and virtue; but so surely as he enters, misfortune, bound to him by his enemy, as a corpse to a living body, enters with him; the wretch who has received his influence, becomes poor, helpless and deserted; happy if he be not burnt at the stake, whipt with iron, torn with red-hot pincers.

"The Spirit of Evil chose a nation for his own; the Spirit of Good tried to redeem that nation from its gulph of vice and misery; and was cruelly destroyed by it; and now, as the masterpiece of the enemy, they are adored together; and he the beneficent, kind and suffering, is made the mediator to pull down curses upon us.

"How quick and secure are the deeds of the evil spirit; how slow and uncertain those of the good! I remember once a good and learned friend of mine telling me that the country about Athens was adorned by the most exquisite works man had ever produced; marble temples traced with divine sculpture, statues transcending human beauty; the art of man had been exhausted to embellish it, the lives of hundreds of men had been wasted to accomplish it, the genius of the wisest had been employed in its execution; ages had passed, while slowly, year by year, these wonders had been collected; some were almost falling through exceeding age, while others shone in their first infancy. Well:—a king, Philip of Macedon, destroyed all these in three days, burnt them, razed them, annihilated them. This is the proportionate energy of good and evil; the produce of ages is the harvest of a moment; a man may spend years in curbing his passions, in acquiring wisdom, in becoming an angel in excellence; the brutality of a fellow creature, or the chance of war, may fell him in an instant; and all his knowledge and virtues become blank, as a moonless, starless night.

"Euthanasia, my heart aches, and my spirits flag: I was a poor, simple girl; but I have suffered much; and endurance, and bitter experience have let me into the truth of things; the deceitful veil which is cast over this world, is powerless to hide its deformity from me. I see the cruel heart, which lurks beneath the beautiful skin of the pard; I see the blight of autumn in the green leaves of spring, the wrinkles of age in the face of youth, rust on the burnished iron, storm in the very breast of calm, sorrow in the heart of joy; all beauty wraps deformity, as the fruit the kernel; Time opens the shell, the seed is poison."

The eyes of Beatrice shot forth sparks of fire as she poured out this anathema against the creation; her cheeks were fevered with a hectic glow; her voice, sharp and broken, which was sometimes raised almost to a shriek, and sometimes lowered to a whisper, fell on the brain of Euthanasia like a rain of alternate fire and ice; she shrunk and trembled beneath the flood of terror that inundated and confounded her understanding: but the eloquent prophetess of Evil ceased at last, and, pale and exhausted, she sank down; clasping Euthanasia in her arms, she hid her face on her knees, and sobbed, and wept:"Forgive me, if I have said that which appears to you blasphemy; I will unveil my heart to you, tell you my sufferings, and surely you will then curse with me the author of my being."

Euthanasia spoke consolation alone; she bade her weep no more; that she need no longer fear or hate; that she might again love, hope and trust; and that she as a tender sister would sympathize with and support her. The undisciplined mind of poor Beatrice was as a flower that droops beneath the storm; but, on the first gleam of sunshine, raises again its head, even though the hail-stones and the wind might have broken and tarnished its leaves and its tints. She looked up, and smiled; "I will do all that you tell me; I will be docile, good and affectionate;—I will be obedient to your smallest sign, kindest, dearest Euthanasia. Trust me, you shall make me a Catholic again, if you will love me unceasingly for one whole year, and in the mean time

I do not die. I am very teachable, very, very tractable; but I have suffered greatly, as one day you will know; for I will tell you every thing. Now, good bye; I am very tired, and I think I shall sleep."

"Sleep then, poor creature; here is a couch ready for you; I will watch near you; and may your dreams be pleasant."

"Give me your hand then; I will hold it while I rest; how small, and white, and soft it is! Look at mine, it is yellow and dry; once it was like yours; I think it was rather smaller, but never so well shaped; the tips of my fingers and my nails were never dyed by so roseate a tint as this, nor was the palm so silken soft. You are very beautiful, and very good, dear Euthanasia; I hope you are, and will be happy."

Euthanasia kissed the forehead of this child of imagination and misery; and soon she slept, forgetful of all her sufferings. Euthanasia felt deeply interested in her; she felt that they were bound together, by their love for one who loved only himself; she thought over her wild denunciations; and, strange to say, she felt doubly warmed with admiration of the creation, and gratitude towards God, at the moment that Beatrice had painted its defects. She thought of the beauty of the world and the wondrous nature of man, until her mind was raised to an enthusiastic sentiment of happiness and praise. "And you also shall curb your wild thoughts," whispered Euthanasia, as she looked at the sleeping girl; "I will endeavour to teach you the lessons of true religion; and, in reducing the wandering thoughts of one so lovely and so good, I shall be in part fulfilling my task on the earth."

For several days after this conversation Beatrice became ·peaceful and mild, saying little, and appearing complacent, almost content; she attended mass, told her beads, and talked of going to confession. Euthanasia was astounded; she was herself so steady in her principles, so firm in opinion and action, slow to change, but resolute having changed, that she was at a loss to understand the variable feelings and swift mutations of the poor, untaught Beatrice.

"Confess!" she repeated; "you promised that I should convert you in a year; but you have already forsaken your Paterin opinions!"

"No, indeed, I have not; but it is of so little consequence; I would please you, dearest, by seeming what I am not; not that I am sure that I am not what you desire. You know, if God is good, he will forgive my errors: if he is evil, I care not to please him; so I shall endeavour to please the virtuous and kind of this world, and you are one of those, my best friend. Besides, now I think of it, this world seems too beautiful to have been created by an evil spirit; he would have made us all toads, the trees and flowers all mushrooms, and the rocks and mountains would have been huge, formless polypi. Yet there is evil; but I will not trouble myself more about it; you shall form my creed; and, as a lisping infant, with clasped hands, I will repeat my prayers after you."

"Why so, dearest Beatrice? Why will you not recal the creeds of your childhood, as your adoptive parents taught them you? I cannot school you better than they."

"My childhood!" cried the prophetess; her eyes becoming dark and stormy, "what to become again a dupe, a maniac? to fall again, as I have fallen? Cease, cease, in mercy cease, to talk of my childhood; days of error, vanity and paradise! My lessons must all be new; all retold in words signifying other ideas than what they signified during my mad, brief dream of youth. Then faith was not a shadow: it was what these eyes saw; I clutched hope, and found it certainty; I heard the angels of heaven, and saw the souls of the departed; can I ever see them again?"

"Sweetest and most unfortunate, drive away memory, and take hope to you. Youth is indeed a dream; and, if I spent it not in your extacies, yet believe me I was not then as I am now. I am older than you, and know life better; I have passed the fearful change from dream to reality, and am now calm. I have known all your throes; sometimes indeed they now visit me; but I quench them, cast them aside, tread on them;—so may you."

"Never! never!" replied Beatrice: "I was born for wretchedness. When the fates twined my destiny, they mingled three threads; the first was green hope, the second purple joy, the third black despair; but the two first were very short, and soon came to an end; a dreary line of black alone remains. Yet I would forget all that; and for many days I have been as calm as a bird that broods, rocked on her tree by a gentle wind; full of a quiet, sleepy life. Should this state continue longer, I might become what you wish me to be; but I find my soul awakening, and I fear a relapse; I fear the return of tears and endless groans. Oh! let me wrap myself round you, my better angel, hope of my life; pour your balmy words upon me; lay your cool, healthful cheek near my burning one, let our pulses beat responsive! Oh! that once I could become less feverish, less wild; less like a dark and crimsoned thunder-cloud, driven away, away, through the unknown wildernesses of sky."

Euthanasia was glad to hear her suffering friend talk, however wildly; for she observed that, when she had exhausted herself in speech, she became calmer and happier; while, if she brooded silently over her cares, she became almost insane through grief. Occasionally she sought consolation in music; there was something magical in her voice, and in the tones she could draw from the organ or the harp: in her days of glory it had been said, that she was taught to sing by angelic instructors; and now those remembered melodies remained, sole relics of her faded honours. The recollection of this sometimes disturbed her; and she would suddenly break off her song, and peevishly exclaim, that music, like the rest of the world's masks, contained the soul of bitterness within its form of beauty.

"Not so, dear girl," said Euthanasia; "Euterpe has ever been so dear a friend of mine, that I cannot permit you to calumniate her unjustly; there is to me an unalloyed pleasure in music. Some blessed spirit, compassionate of man's estate, and loving him, sent it, to teach him that he is other than what he seems: it comes, like a voice from a far world, to tell you that there are depths of intense emotion veiled in the blue empyrean, and the windows of heaven are opened by music alone. It chastens and lulls our extacies; and, if it awakens grief, it also soothes it. But more than to the happy or the sorrowful, music is an inestimable gift to those who forget all sublimer emotions in the pursuits of daily life. I listen to the talk of men; I play with my embroidery-frame; I enter into society: suddenly high song awakens me, and I leave all this tedious routine far, far distant; I listen, till all the world is changed, and the beautiful earth becomes more beautiful. Evening and all its soft delights, morning and all its refreshing loveliness;—noonday, when the busy soul rests, like the sun in its diurnal course, and then gathering new strength, descends; all these, when thought upon, bring pleasure; but music is far more delicious than these. Never do I feel happier and better, than when I have heard sweet music; my thoughts often sleep like young children nestled in their cradles, until music awakens them, and they open their starry eyes. I may be mistaken; but music seems to me to reveal to us some of the profoundest secrets of the universe; and the spirit, freed from prison by its charms, can then soar, and gaze with eagle eyes on the eternal sun of this all-beauteous world."

Beatrice smiled.—Since her days of happiness had ended, Euthanasia's enthusiasm had become more concentrated, more concealed; but Beatrice again awoke her to words, and these two ladies, bound by the sweet ties of gratitude and pity, found in each other's converse some balm for their misfortunes. Circumstances had thus made friends of those whom nature seemed to separate: they were much unlike; but the wild looks of Beatrice sometimes reflected the soft light of Euthanasia's eyes; and Euthanasia found her heart, which was sinking to apathy, awake again, as she listened to Beatrice. And, though we may be unhappy, we can never be perfectly wretched, while the mind is active; it is inaction alone that constitutes true wretchedness.

In the mean time her own journey to Florence was put off indefinitely. She was too much interested in the fate of Beatrice, and already loved her too well, to desert her; the poor prophetess appeared little capable of the journey, since the most trifling circumstance would awaken her wildest fancies, and fever and convulsions followed. Once indeed Euthanasia had mentioned her wish to go thither; Beatrice looked at her with flashing eyes, and cried, "Did you not promise never to desert me? Are you faithless also?"

"But would you not accompany me?"

"Do you see that river that flows near Lucca?" exclaimed Beatrice. "I fancy that it has flowed through the self-same banks these many thousand years; and sooner will it desert them, than I this town. See you that cypress, that grows towering above all its neighbour trees in that convent-garden, I am as firm to this soil as that; I will never leave this place but by force, and then I die."

She said these words in her wildest manner; and they were followed by such an annihilation of strength, and such symptoms of fever, that Euthanasia did not again dare mention her removal to Florence. She also suffered less by her continued stay at Lucca; for the feelings of her heart were so completely absorbed in pity and love for Beatrice, that the painful ideas of many years' growth seemed rooted out by a new and mightier power. She was so little selfish, that she could easily forget her own sorrows, deep as they were, in her sympathy for the unhappy prophetess, who had suffered evils tremendous and irremediable.

Castruccio often sent to learn of the welfare of this poor girl, and Euthanasia answered his enquiries with exactness. She did this; for she thought that perhaps the future destiny of Beatrice was in his hands, and that he might engraft life and even happiness on the blighted plant.

One day Beatrice went out. It was the first time she had quitted the palace; and Euthanasia was vexed and anxious. After an absence of some hours she returned; she was clothed in a great coarse cloak that entirely disguised her; she put it off; and, trembling, blushing, panting, she threw herself into the arms of her protectress.

"I have seen him! I have seen him!"

"Calm yourself, poor fluttering bird; you have seen him: well, well, he is changed, much altered; why do you weep?"

"Aye, he is changed; but he is far more beautiful than ever he was. Oh, Euthanasia, how radiant, how divine he is! His eyes, which, like the eagle's, could outgaze the sun, yet melt in the sweetest love, as a cloud, shining, yet soft; his brow, manly and expansive, on which his raven curls rest; his upturned lips, where pride, and joy, and love, and wisdom, and triumph live, small spirits, ready to obey his smallest will; and his head, cinctured by a slight diadem, looks carved out by the intensest knowledge of beauty! How graceful his slightest motion! and his voice,—his voice is here,——"

Beatrice put her hand upon her heart; her eyes were filled with tears; and the whole expression of her face was softened and humanized. Suddenly she stopped; she dried her eyes; and, fixing them on Euthanasia, she took her two hands in hers, and looked on her, as if she would read her soul. "Beautiful creature," she said, "once he told me that he loved you. Did he not? does he not? Why are you separated? do you not love him?"

"I did; once I did truly; but he has cast off that which was my love; and, like a flower plucked from the stalk, it has withered—as you see it."

"Aye, that is strange. What did he cast off?"

"Why will you make me speak? He cast off humanity, honesty, honourable feeling, all that I prize."

"Forms, forms,—mere forms, my mistaken Euthanasia. *He* remained, and was not that every thing? Methinks, it would please me, that my lover should cast off all humanity, and be a reprobate, and an outcast of his species. Oh! then how deeply and tenderly I should love him; soiled with crimes, his hands dripping blood, I would shade him as the flowering shrub invests the ruin; I would cover him with a spotless veil;—my intensity of love would annihilate his wickedness;—every one would hate him;—but, if all adored him, it would not come near the sum of my single affection. I should be every thing to him, life, and hope; he would die in his remorse; but he would live again and again in the light of my love; I would invest him as a silvery mist, so that none should see how evil he was; I would pour out before him large draughts of love, that he should become drunk with it, until he grew good and kind. So you deserted this glorious being, and he has felt the pangs of unrequited affection, the helpless throes of love cast as water upon the sand of the desert? Oh, indeed I pity him!"

"Believe me," cried Euthanasia, "he has other affections. Glory and conquest are his mistresses, and he is a successful lover; already he has deluged our vallies in blood, and turned our habitations into black and formless ruins; he has torn down the banners of the Florentines, and planted his own upon the towers of noble cities; I believe him to be happy."

"Thank God for that; I would pour out my blood, drop by drop, to make him happy. But he is not married, and you have deserted him; I love him; he has loved me; is it impossible—? Oh! foolish, hateful wretch that I am, what do I say? No creature was ever so utterly undone!"

Beatrice covered her face with her hands; her struggles were violent; she shrunk from Euthanasia's consoling embrace; and at length, quite overcome, she sank in convulsions on the pavement of the hall. Her paroxysm was long and fearful; it was succeeded by a heavy lethargic sleep; during the first part of which she was feverish and uneasy; but, after some hours, her cheeks became pale, her pulse beat slower, and her breath was drawn regularly.

Euthanasia watched beside her alone: when she found that she was sleeping quietly and deeply, she retired from her bedside; and, sitting at some distance, she tried to school herself on the bitter feelings that had oppressed her since the morning. Euthanasia was so self-examining, that she never allowed a night to elapse without recalling her feelings and actions of the past day; she endeavoured to be simply just to herself, and her soul had so long been accustomed to this discipline, that it easily laid open its dearest secrets. Misfortune had not dulled her sense of right and wrong; her understanding was still clear, though tinged by the same lofty enthusiasm which had ever been her characteristic. She now searched her soul to find what were the feelings which still remained to her concerning Castruccio; she hardly knew whether it was hate or love. Hate! could she hate one, to whom once she had delivered up all her thoughts, as to the tribunal of her God, whom she had loved as one to whom she was willing to unite herself for ever? And could she love one, who had deceived her in her dearest hopes, who had lulled her on the brink of a precipice, to plunge her with greater force to eternal unhappiness? She felt neither hatred, nor revenge, nor contempt colder than either; she felt grief alone, and that sentiment was deeply engraven on her soul.

CHAPTER IV

She was awakened from this reverie by the voice of Beatrice, who called to her to come near. "I am quite recovered," she said, "though weak; I have been very ill to-day, and I am frightened to think of the violence of my sensations. But sit near me, beloved friend; it is now night, and you will hear no sound but my feeble voice; while I fulfil my promise of relating to you my wretched history."

"Mine own Beatrice, do not now vex yourself with these recollections; you must seek calm and peace alone; let memory go to its grave."

"Nay, you must know all," replied Beatrice, peevishly; "why do you balk me? indeed I do best when I follow my own smallest inclinations; for, when I try to combat them, I am again ill, as I was this morning. Sit beside me; I will make room for you on my couch; give me your hand, but turn away your soft eyes; and now I will tell you every thing.

"You know that I loved Castruccio; how much I need hardly tell: I loved him beyond human love, for I thought heaven itself had interfered to unite us. I thought——alas! it is with aching pain that I recollect my wild dreams,—that we two were chosen from the rest of the world, gifted with celestial faculties. It appeared to me to be a dispensation of Providence, that I should have met him at the full height of my glory, when I was burning with triumph and joy. I do not think, my own Euthanasia, that you can ever have experienced the vigour and fire of my sensations. Victory in an almost desperate struggle, success in art, love itself, are earthly feelings, subject to change and death; but, when these three most exquisite sensations are bestowed by the visible intervention of heaven, thus giving security to the unstable, and eternity to what is fleeting, such an event fills the over-brimming cup, intoxicates the brain, and renders her who feels them more than mortal.

"Victory and glory I had, and an assurance of divine inspiration; the fame of what I was, was spread among the people of my country; then love came, and flattered, and softened, and overcame me. Well, that I will pass over: to conceive that all I felt was human, common, and now faded, disgusts me, and makes me look back with horror to my lost paradise. Castruccio left me; and I sat I cannot tell how long, white, immoveable, and intranced; hours, I believe days, passed; I cannot tell, for in truth I think I was mad.

Yet I was silent; not a word, not a tear, not a sound escaped me, until some one mentioned the name of Castruccio before me, and then I wept. I did not rave or weep aloud; I crept about like a shadow, brooding over my own thoughts, and trying to divine the mystery of my destiny.

"At length I went to my good father, the bishop; I knelt down before him: 'Rise, dear child,' he said; 'how pale you are! what has quenched the fire of your brilliant eyes?'

"'Father, holy father,' I replied, 'I will not rise till you answer me one question.'—My looks were haggard with want of rest; my tangled locks fell on my neck; my glazed eyes could scarcely distinguish any object.

"'My blessed Beatrice,' said the good old man, 'you are much unlike yourself: but speak; I know that you can ask nothing that I can refuse to tell.'

"'Tell me then, by your hopes of heaven,' I cried, 'whether fraud was used in the *Judgement of God* that I underwent, or how I escaped the fearful burning of the hot shares.'

"Tears started in my father's eyes; he rose, and embraced me, and, lifting me up, said with passion,—'Thank God! my prayers are fulfilled. Beatrice, you shall not be deceived, you will no longer deceive yourself; and do not be unhappy, but joy that the deceit is removed from you, and that you may return from your wild and feverish extacies to a true and real piety.'

"'This is all well,' I replied calmly; 'but tell me truly how it happened.'

"'That I cannot, my child, for I was myself kept in the dark; I only know that fraud was most certainly practised for your deliverance. My child, we have all of us much erred; you less than any; for you have been deceived, led away by your feelings and imagination to believe yourself that which you are not.'

"I will not repeat to you all that the bishop said; it was severe, but kind. First he shewed me, how I had deceived myself, and nourished extacies and transports of the soul which were in no way allied to holiness; and then he told me how I must repair my faults by deep humility, prayer, and a steady faith in that alone which others taught, not what I myself imagined. I listened silently; but I heard every word; I was very docile; I believed all he said; and although my soul bled with its agony, I accused none, none but myself. At first I thought that I would tell my countrymen of their deception. But, unsupported by my supernatural powers, I now shrunk from all display; no veil, no wall could conceal me sufficiently; for it could not hide me from myself. My very powers of speech deserted me, and I could not articulate a syllable; I listened, my eyes bent on the earth, my cheek pale; I listened until I almost became marble. At length the good old man ceased; and, with many words of affectionate comfort, he bade me go and make firm peace with my own heart, and that then he hoped to teach me a calm road to happiness. Happiness! surely I must have been stone; for I neither frowned in despite, nor laughed in derision, when that term was applied to any thing that I could hereafter feel. I kissed his hand, and withdrew.

"Did you ever feel true humility? a prostration of soul, that accuses itself alone, and asks pardon of a superior power with entire penitence, and a confiding desertion of all self-merit, a persuasion intimate and heartfelt of one's own unworthiness? That was what I felt; I had been vain, proud, presumptuous; now I fell to utter poverty of spirit; yet it was not poverty, for there was a richness in my penitence, which reminded me of the sacred text, that says 'Oh, that my head were water, and mine eyes a fountain of tears!'

"Then succeeded to this mental humiliation, a desire to mortify and punish myself for my temerity and mistakes. I was possessed by a spirit of martyrdom. Sometimes I thought that I would again undergo the *Judgement of God* fairly and justly: but now I shrunk from public exhibition; besides, the good bishop had strongly reprobated these temptations of God's justice. At other times I thought that I would confess all to my excellent father; and this perhaps is what I ought to have done; what would really have caused me to regain a part of the calm that I had lost; but I could not; womanly shame forbade me; death would have been a far preferable alternative. At length an idea struck me, that seemed to my overstrained feelings to transcend all other penitence; a wretchedness and anguish that might well redeem my exceeding sins.

"Think you that, while I thus humbled myself, I forgot Castruccio? Never! the love I bore him clung around me, festered on my soul, and kept me ever alive to pain. Love him! I adored him; to whisper his name only in solitude, where none could hear my voice but my own most attentive ear, thrilled me with transport. I tried to banish him my thoughts; he recurred in my dreams, which I could not control. I saw him there, beautiful as his real self, and my heart was burnt by my emotion. Well; it was on this excess of love that I built my penitence, which was to go as a pilgrim and ask alms of you. Euthanasia! I only knew your name; the very idea of seeing you made me shiver. I was three months before I could steel my heart to this resolve. I saw none; I spoke to none; I was occupied by my meditations alone, and those were deep and undermining as the ocean.

"Well; as I have said, I dwelt long and deeply upon my plan, until every moment seemed a crime, that went by before I put it in execution. The long winter passed thus; my poor mother, the lady Marchesana, watched me, as a child might watch a favourite bird fluttering in the agonies of death. She saw that some mysterious and painful feeling oppressed me, that I no longer appeared in public, that I shunned the worship of my admirers, that the spirit of prophecy was dead within me; but I was silent, and reserved; and her reverence for me (Good angels! her reverence for me!) prevented any enquiries. In the spring the bishop Marsilio was promoted to another see, and he was obliged to go to Avignon to receive the investiture. Excellent and beloved old man! he blessed me, and kissed me, and with words of affectionate advice departed. I have never seen him more.

"When he was gone, the labour of my departure was lightened; and in gentle and hesitating words I told my best and loved mother that I had vowed a pilgrimage to Rome: she wished to accompany me. Those were heart-breaking scenes, my Euthanasia, when I left all my friends, all who loved me, and whom I had ever loved: I knew that I should never see them again. How did I know this? In truth, after having performed my vow with regard to you, I intended to visit the sepulchres at Rome; and I might then have returned. I was no prophetess; and yet I felt that mine was not a simple pilgrimage, but an eternal separation from all former associations, from every one I had ever known. Thus, hopeless of future good, I deserted all that yet rendered life in any degree sufferable: I did this to satisfy my sense of duty, to do homage to the divinity by some atonement for his violated laws: I did this; and henceforward I was to be an outcast, a poor lonely shrub on a bleak heath, a single reed in a vast and overflowing river.

"I had known too much luxury in my youth; every one loved me, and tended on me; I had seen about me eyes beaming with affection, smiles all my own, words of deep interest and respect, that had become to me a second nature. I departed alone at four in the morning from Ferrara by the secret entrance of the viscountess's palace, on a clear and lovely day in the spring. I was dressed as the meanest pilgrim, and I carefully hid my white hands and fair cheeks, which might have betrayed my way of life during the past; except indeed when I was alone,—then I loved to throw off my cloak, to bare my arms, my face, my neck to the scorching sun-beams, that I might the sooner destroy a delicacy I despised: the work was quickly done; a few hours exposure to the sun of noon burnt up my skin, and made it red and common.

"The first day was one of unmixed pain; the sun parched my frame; my feet were blistered, my limbs ached; I walked all day, until bodily fatigue lulled my mental anguish, for I was unhappy beyond all words. Alone, deserted by God and man, I had lost my firm support, my belief in my own powers; I had lost my friends; and I found, that the vain, self-sufficing, cloud-inhabiting Beatrice was in truth a poor dependent creature, whose heart sunk, when in the evening she came to a clear brook running through a little wood, and she found no cup to drink, and no dainties to satisfy her appetite. I dragged my weary limbs three miles further, to an hospital for pilgrims, and repined over my coarse fare and coarser bed:—I, the ethereal prophetess, who fancied that I could feed upon air and beautiful thoughts, who had regarded my body but as a servant to my will, to hunger and thirst only as I bade it.

"Alone! alone! I travelled on day after day, in short, but wearisome journeys, and I felt the pain of utter and forced solitude; the burning sun shone, and the dews fell at evening, but there was no breeze, no coolness to refresh me; the nights were close, and my limbs, dried with the scorching of the day, and stiff with walking, burned all night as if a furnace had glowed within them. Were these slight evils? Alas! I was a spoiled child, and I felt every pain as an agony.

"I fell ill; I caught cold one evening, when just after sunset I threw myself down to rest under a tree, and the unwholesome dew fell upon me. I got a low fever, which for a long time I did not understand, feeling one day well, and the next feverish, cold, and languid. Some attendant nuns at an hospital found out my disorder, and nursed me; I was confined for six weeks; and, when I issued forth, little of the fire of my eyes, or of the beauty the lady Marchesana used to dwell upon, out-lived this attack.—I was yellow, meagre,——a shadow of what I had been.

"My journey to your castle was very long. I crossed the Apennines during the summer, and passing through Florence I arrived at Pistoia in the beginning of June. But now my heart again failed; I heard of your name, your prosperity, your beauty, the respect and adoration you every where excited: it was a double penance to humble myself before so excelling a rival. If you had been worthless, a self-contenting pride would have eased my wounds, but to do homage to my equal—oh! to one far my superior,—was a new lesson to my stubborn soul. I remained nearly three months at Pistoia, very unhappy, hesitating,—cast about, as a boat that for ever shifts its sail, but can never find the right wind to lead it into port.

"I visited you in September; do you remember my coming? do you remember my hesitating gait, and low and trembling voice? I was giddy—sick—I thought that death was upon me, for that nothing but that great change could cause such an annihilation of my powers, such an utter sinking of my spirit. A cold dew stood upon my forehead, my eyes were glazed and sightless, my limbs trembled as with convulsions. Castruccio loved you! Castruccio! it is long since I have mentioned his name: during this weary journey never did his loved image for a moment quit its temple, its fane, its only home, that it still and for ever fills. Love him! it was madness; yet I did;—yet I do;—put your hand upon my heart,—does it not beat fast?"

Euthanasia kissed poor Beatrice's forehead; and, after a short pause, she continued:

"My penance was completed, yet I did not triumph; an unconquerable sadness hung over me; miserable dreams haunted my sleep; and their recollected images strayed among my day-thoughts, as thin and grim ghosts, frightening and astounding me. Once,—I can never forget,—I had been oppressed for several days by an overpowering and black melancholy, for which I could in no manner account; it was not regret or grief; it was a sinking, an annihilation of all my mental powers in which I was a passive sufferer, as if the shadow of some mightier spirit was cast over to darken and depress me. I was haunted as by a prophecy, or rather a sense of evil, which I could neither define nor understand. Three evenings after, as I sat beside a quiet spring that lulled me almost to insensibility, the cause of my mournful reveries suddenly flashed across me; it stalked on my recollection, as a terrific and gigantic shadow, and made me almost die with terror. The memory of a dream flashed across me. Again and again I have dreamed this dream, and always on the eve of some great misfortune. It is my genius, my dæmon. What was it? there was something said, something done, a scene pourtrayed. Listen attentively, I intreat; there was a wide plain flooded by the waters of an overflowing river, the road was dry, being on the side of a hill above the level of the plain, and I kept along the path which declined, wondering if I should come to an insurmountable obstacle; at a distance before me they were driving a flock of sheep; on my left, on the side of the hill, there was a ruined circuit of wall, which inclosed the dilapidated houses of a deserted town; at some distance a dreary, large, ruinous house, half like a castle, yet without a tower, dilapidated, and overgrown with moss, was dimly seen, islanded by the flood on which it cast a night-black shade; the scirocco blew, and covered the sky with fleecy clouds; and the mists in the distance hovered low over the plain; a bat above me wheeled around. Then something happened, what I cannot now tell, terrific it most certainly was; Euthanasia, there is something in this strange world, that we none of us understand.

"Euthanasia, I came to that scene; if I live, I did! I saw it all as I had before seen it in the slumbers of the night. Great God, what am I? I am frailer than the first autumnal leaf that falls; I am overpowered."

She paused sobbing with passion; a clinging horror fell upon Euthanasia; they were for a long time silent, and then Beatrice in a low subdued voice continued:

"I had returned to Florence; I had passed through Arezzo; I had left Thrasymene to the north; I had passed through Perugia, Foligno, and Terni, and was descending towards the plain surrounding Rome; the Tiber had overflowed, the whole of the low country was under water; but I proceeded, descending the mountains, until, having passed Narni, I came to the lowest hill which bounds the Campagna di Roma; the scirocco blew; the mists were on the hills, and half concealed the head of lone Soracte; the white waters, cold and dreary, were spread far, waste and shelterless; on my left was a high dark wall surrounding a ruined town—I looked,—some way beyond I saw on the road a flock of sheep almost lost in the distance,—my brain was troubled, I grew dizzy and sick—when my glazed eyes caught a glance of an old, large, dilapidated house islanded in the flood,—the dream flashed across my memory; I uttered a wild shriek, and fell lifeless on the road.

"I again awoke, but all was changed: I was lying on a couch, in a vast apartment, whose loose tapestries waved and sighed in the wind;—near me were two boys holding torches which flared, and their black smoke was driven across my eyes; an old woman was chafing my temples.—I turned my head from the light of the torches, and then I first saw my wicked and powerful enemy: he leaned against the wall, observing me; his eyes had a kind of fascination in them, and, unknowing what I did, hardly conscious that he was a human creature, (indeed for a time it appeared to me only a continuation of my dream,) I gazed on his face, which became illuminated by a proud triumphant, fiendlike smile.—I felt sick at heart, and relapsed into a painful swoon.

"Well: I promised to be brief, and I go on dwelling on the particulars of my tale, until your fair cheek is blanched still whiter by fear. But I have said enough, nor will I tell that which would chill your warm blood with horror. I remained three years in this house; and what I saw, and what I endured, is a tale for the unhallowed ears of infidels, or for those who have lost humanity in the sight of blood, and not for so tender a heart as yours. It has changed me, much changed me, to have been witness of these scenes; I entered young, I came out grey, old and withered; I went in innocent; and, if innocence consist in ignorance, I am now guilty of the knowledge of crime, which it would seem that fiends alone could contrive.

"What was he, who was the author and mechanist of these crimes? he bore a human name; they say that his lineage was human; yet could he be a man? During the day he was absent; at night he returned, and his roofs rung with the sounds of festivity, mingled with shrieks and imprecations. It was the carnival of devils, when we miserable victims were dragged out to——

"Enough! enough! Euthanasia, do you wonder that I, who have been the slave of incarnate Evil, should have become a Paterin?

"That time has passed as a dream. Often my faculties were exerted to the utmost; my energies alive, at work, combating;—but I struggled against victory, and was ever vanquished. I have seen the quiet stars shine, and the shadow of the grated window of the hall lie upon the moon-enlightened pavement, and it crawled along silently as I had observed it in childhood, so that truly I inhabited the same world as you,—yet how different! Animal life was the same; the household dog knew, and was at last obedient to my voice; the cat slumbered in the sun;—what was the influence that hung alone over the mind of man, rendering it cruel, hard and fiendlike?

"And who was the author of these ills? There was something about him that might be called beautiful; but it was the beauty of the tiger, of lightning, of the cataract that destroys. Obedience waited on his slightest motion; for he made none, that did not command; his followers worshipped him, but it was as a savage might worship the god of evil. His slaves dared not murmur;— his eyes beamed with irresistible fire, his smile was as death. I hated him; and I alone among his many victims was not quelled to submission. I cursed him—I poured forth eloquent and tumultuous maledictions on his head, until I changed his detested love into less dreadful, less injurious hate. Yet then I did not escape; his boiling and hideous passions, turned to revenge, now endeavoured to wreak themselves in my misery. These limbs, my Euthanasia, have been wrenched in tortures; cold, famine and thirst have kept like blood-hounds a perpetual watch upon my wearied life; yet I still live to remember and to curse.

"But, though life survived these rending struggles, my reason sank beneath them!—I became mad. Oh! dearest friend, may you never know what I suffered, when I perceived the shadow of a false vision overpower me, and my sickening throes, when the bars of my dungeon, its low roof, and black thick air, would, as it were, peer upon me with a stifling sense of reality amidst my insane transports. I struggled to recall my reason, and to preserve it; I wept, I prayed;—but I was again lost; and the fire that dwelt in my brain gave unnatural light to every object. But I must speak of that no more; methinks I again feel, what it is madness only to recollect.

"I told you that I remained for three years in this infernal house. You can easily imagine how slowly the days and nights succeeded one to another, each adding to my age, each adding one misery more to my list. Still I was the slave of him, who was a man in form alone, and of his companions, who, if they did not equal him in malice, yet were more vile, more treacherous, than he. At length the Pope's party besieged the castle. The many crimes of its possessor had drawn on him the hatred of the country round; and the moment that a leader appeared, the whole peasantry flocked as to a crusade to destroy their oppressor. He was destroyed. I saw him die, calm, courageous and unrepenting. I stood alone near his couch of blood-stained cloaks thrown in a heap upon the floor, on which when he staggered into the room he had fallen; he asked me for a cup of water; I raised his head, and gave him to drink; he said—'I feel new strength, I shall be better soon.' And, saying those words, he died.

"I was now free. I arose from the floor on which I knelt; and dividing from my eyes my hair dabbled in his blood, I cut off with his dagger the long and dripping locks, and threw them on his body. I disguised me in the clothes of one of his pages, and hid myself, until by the submission of his followers the outlet from my prison should be free. As I said before, it was more a vast palace than a castle, being without towers or battlements; but it was fortified by numberless ditches and other obstacles, apparently small, yet which, defended by slingers and archers, became almost impregnable. But when the chief died, these were deserted; and the partners of his rapine and his feasts filled the air with their savage lamentations. The fortress was taken; and I escaped to the mountains, the wild, wild mountains,—I sought them as a home after my long and painful imprisonment.

"I was now free. The ilex trees shaded me; the waters murmured beside me; the sweet winds passed over my cheeks. I felt new life. I was no longer a haggard prisoner, the despairing victim of others' crimes, the inhabitant of the dark and blood-stained walls of a house, which hedged me in on all sides, and interrupted the free course of my health even in sleep. I was again Beatrice; I again felt the long absent sensations of joy: it was paradise to me, to see the stars of heaven, unimpeded by the grates of my dungeon-windows, to walk, to rest, to think, to speak, uninterrupted and unheard. I became delirious with joy; I embraced the rough trunks of the old trees, as if they were my sisters in freedom and delight;—I took up in my hand the sparkling waters of the stream, and scattered them to the winds;—I threw myself on the earth, I kissed the rocks, I raved with tumultuous pleasure. Free! free! I can run, until my strength fails; I can rest on a mossy bank, until my strength returns; I hear the waving of the branches; I see the flight of the birds; I can lie on the grassy floor of my mother-earth so long unvisited; and I can call nature my own again. It was autumn, and the underwood of the forest had strewn the ground with its withered leaves; the arbutus-berries, chesnuts, and other fruits satisfied my appetite. I felt no want, no fatigue; the common shapes of this world seemed arrayed in unusual loveliness, to welcome and feast me on my new-found liberty.

"I wandered many days, and penetrated into the wild country of the Abruzzi. But I was again lost: I know not what deprived me of reason thus, when I most needed it. Whether it were the joy, or the sudden change, attendant on a too intense sensation of freedom, which made me feel as if I interpenetrated all nature, alive and boundless. I have recollections, as if sometimes I saw the woods, the green earth, and blue sky, and heard the roaring of a mighty waterfal which splashed me with its cold waters: but there is a blank, as of a deep, lethargic sleep; and many weeks passed before I awoke again, and entered upon the reality of life.

"I found myself in a cavern lying on the ground. It was night; and a solitary lamp burned, fastened to the wall of the cave; the half-extinguished ashes of a fire glimmered in a recess; and a few utensils that appeared to have been intended for the preparing food, seemed to mark this as a human habitation. It was dry, and furnished with a few benches and a table, on which lay bread and fruits. I felt as if I had become the inhabitant of the dwelling of a spirit; and, with a strange, half-painful, half-pleasurable feeling, I raised an apple to my lips, that by its fragrance and taste I might assure myself that it was earthly. Then again I looked around for some fellow-creature. I found a narrow passage from my cave, which led to an inner apartment much smaller and very low; on the ground, on a bed of leaves lay an old man: his grey hairs were thinly strewn on his venerable temples, his beard white, flowing and soft, fell to his girdle; he smiled even in his sleep a gentle smile of benevolence. I knelt down beside him; methought it was my excellent father, the lord Marsilio; but that there were greater traces of thought and care upon the fallen cheeks and wrinkled brow of this old man.

"He awoke: 'My poor girl,' he said, 'what would you?'

"'I wish to know where I am, and what I do here?'

"My words convinced my good protector, that the kindly sleep into which his medicines had thrown me, had restored my reason; and, it being now day-break, he arose, and opened the door of his cave. It was dug under the side of a mountain, covered by ivy, wild vines, and other parasites, and shaded by ilex trees; it opened on the edge of a small grassy platform, with a steep wall of rock behind, and a precipice before: the mountain in which it was scooped, was one of many that inclosed a rugged valley; and, from one spot on the platform, I could distinguish a mass of waters falling with a tremendous crash, which were afterwards hidden by the inequalities of the mountain, and then were seen, a turbid and swift river, at the bottom of the valley. The lower sides of the mountain were covered with olive woods, whose seagreen colour contrasted with the dark ilex, and the fresh-budding leaves of a few chesnuts. I felt cold, and the mountain had just begun to be tipped by the rising sun; it seemed as if no path led to or from the platform, and that we were shut out from the whole world, suspended on the side of a rocky mountain.

"This cavern had been an hospital for me during the long winter months. The old man had found me straying wildly among the forests, complaining of the heavy chains that bound me, and the wrongs and imprisonment that I suffered. He, poor wretch, was an outcast of his species, a heretic, a Paterin, who hid himself in the woods from the fury of the priests who would have destroyed him. He led me to his cave; he tended me as the kindest father; he restored me to reason, and even then did not desert me. He lived here quite alone; no one was intrusted with the secret of his retreat; at night, muffled up and disguised, he often went to seek for food, and again hastened back to peace and solitude.

"I partook his solitude for many months: at sunrise we quitted our dwelling, and enjoyed the fresh air, and the view of the sky and the hills, until the sight of the first countryman in the vale below warned us to retire. On moonlight nights we sat there; and, while she, lady of the night, moved slowly above us, and the stars twinkled around, we talked, and, in our conversations of faith, goodness and power, his doctrines unveiled to me, what had before been obscure, and from him I learned that creed which you hold in detestation, but which, believe me, has much to be said in its behalf.

"Look, dear Euthanasia, daylight has made dim the glimmer of your lamp, and bids me remember how often I have forgotten my promise to be brief in my relation; it is now almost finished. I soon greatly loved my kind guardian; he was the gentlest and most amiable of mortals, wise as a Grecian sage, fearless and independent. He died in torture: the bloodhounds hunted him from his den; they bound his aged limbs; they dragged him to the stake. He died without dread, I would fain believe almost without pain. Could these things be, oh, my preserver, best and most excellent of men? It were well befitting, that thou shouldst die thus, and that I lived, and still live.

"It were tedious to relate how all this passed; how I wept and prayed; how I escaped, and, half maddened by this misery, cursed the creation and its cruel laws. The rest is all uninteresting; I was returning from the task of carrying the last legacy of this old man to his daughter at Genoa, when I was seized in this town by the Inquisitors, and cast into prison,— —you know the rest.

"And now, dearest friend, leave me. Having related the events of my past life, it makes me look on towards the future; it is not enough to rise every day, and then lie down to sleep; I would look on what I may become with firmness; I know that no creature in the whole world is so miserable as I; but I have not yet drained the cup of life; something still remains to be done.

"Yet one word, my Euthanasia, of Him who is the law of my life; and yet I dare not say what I thought of saying. You write to him about me sometimes; do you not? You may still; I would not check you in this. In truth he is the master of my fate; and it were well that he knew all that relates to me."

Poor Beatrice then wept bitterly; but she waved her hand in sign that she would be left alone; and Euthanasia retired. She had not slept the whole night, but she felt no inclination to rest. The last words of Beatrice seemed to imply that she wished that Castruccio should know her story; so she sat down, and wrote an abstract of it, while her eyes often filled with tears, as she related the wondrous miseries of the ill-fated prophetess.

CHAPTER V

On the following day Beatrice seemed far more calm. Euthanasia had feared, that the reviving the memory of past sorrows, might awaken the frenzy from which she had before suffered; but it was not so. She had pined for confidence; her heart was too big to close up in secrecy all the mighty store of unhappiness to which it was conscious; but, having now communicated the particulars to another, she felt somewhat relieved. She and Euthanasia walked up and down the overgrown paths of the palace-garden; and, as Beatrice held her friend's hand, after a silence of a few minutes she said:

"I do not like to pry into the secrets of my own heart; and yet I am ever impelled to do it. I was about to compare it to this unweeded garden; but here all is still; and the progress of life, be it beautiful or evil, goes on in peace: in my soul all jars,—one thought strikes against another, and produces most vile discord. Sometimes for a moment this ceases; and would that that state of peace would endure for ever: but, crash!—comes in the stroke of a mightier hand, which destroys all harmony and melody, alas! that may be found in your gentler heart; in mine all recollection of it even is extinct."

"I will tell you how this is, my sweet Beatrice," replied Euthanasia, playfully. "I will tell you what the human mind is; and you shall learn to regulate its various powers. The human soul, dear girl, is a vast cave, in which many powers sit and live. First, Consciousness is as a centinel at the entrance; and near him wait Joy and Sorrow, Love and Hate, and all the quick sensations that through his means gain entrance into our hearts.

"In the vestibule of this cavern, still illumined by the light of day, sit Memory with banded eyes, grave Judgement bearing her scales, and Reason in a lawyer's gown. Hope and Fear dwell there, hand in hand, twin sisters; the first (the elder by some brief moments, of ruddy complexion, firm step, eyes eagerly looking forward, and lips apart in earnest expectation,) would often hurry on to take her seat beside Joy; if she were not held back by Fear, the younger born; who, pale and trembling, would as often fly, if Hope held not her hand, and supported her; her eyes are ever turned back to appeal to Memory, and you may see her heart beat through her dun robe. Religion dwells there also, and Charity, or sometimes in their place, their counterfeits or opposites, Hypocrisy, Avarice and Cruelty.

"Within, excluded from the light of day, Conscience sits, who can see indeed, as an owl, in the dark. His temples are circled by a diadem of thorns, and in his hand he bears a whip; yet his garb is kingly, and his countenance, though severe, majestical.

"But beyond all this there is an inner cave, difficult of access, rude, strange, and dangerous. Few visit this, and it is often barren and empty; but sometimes (like caverns that we read of, which are discovered in the bosoms of the mountains, and exist in beauty, unknown and neglected) this last recess is decorated with the strongest and most wondrous devices;— stalactites of surpassing beauty, stores of unimagined wealth, and silver sounds, which the dropping water makes, or the circulation of the air, felt among the delicate crystals. But here also find abode owls, and bats, and vipers, and scorpions, and other deadly reptiles. This recess receives no light from outward day; nor has Conscience any authority here. Sometimes it is lighted by an inborn light; and then the birds of night retreat, and the reptiles creep not from their holes. But, if this light do not exist, oh! then let those beware who would explore this cave. It is hence that bad men receive those excuses for their crimes, which take the whip from the hand of Conscience, and blunt his sharp crown; it is hence that the daring heretic learns strange secrets. This is the habitation of the madman, when all the powers desert the vestibule, and he, finding no light, makes darkling, fantastic combinations, and lives among them. From thence there is a short path to hell, and the evil spirits pass and repass unreproved, devising their temptations.

"But it is here also that Poetry and Imagination live; it is here that Heroism, and Self-sacrifice, and the highest virtues dwell, and here they find a lore far better than all the lessons of the world; and here dwells the sweet reward of all our toil, Content of Mind, who crowned with roses, and bearing a flower-wreathed sceptre, rules, instead of Conscience, those admitted to her happy dominion."

Euthanasia talked thus, trying to give birth in the mind of Beatrice to calmer ideas; but it was in vain; the poor girl listened, and when her friend had finished, she raised her eyes heavy with tears. "Talk no more in this strain," she said; "every word you utter tells me only too plainly what a lost wretch I am. No content of mind exists for me, no beauty of thought, or poetry; and, if imagination live, it is as a tyrant, armed with fire, and venomed darts, to drive me to despair."

A torrent of tears followed these words; and no caresses or consolation could soothe her.

Soon after, Euthanasia received an answer from Castruccio to the letter in which she had sketched Beatrice's unhappy story. He lamented the misfortunes, which through his means had overwhelmed the poor prophetess. "I know," he continued, "of no refuge or shelter for her, if it be not in your protecting affection. If she were as when I knew her, her own feelings might suggest a cloister, as the last resource for one so outraged and so miserable as she is. But she is a Paterin; and, until she be reclaimed from this detestable heresy, she is shut out from the consolations of our religion."

"And he writes thus coldly of this ruined temple, which was once all that is fair and beautiful! Ah! I wonder not," thought Euthanasia, "that he cast away my affections, since he can spare no deeper sympathy for Beatrice. She does not interfere with his ambition or his designs; it is therefore hardness of heart alone which dictates his chilling councils."

At this moment Beatrice entered. To see that beautiful creature only (for beautiful she still was in spite of calamity and madness), was to behold all that can be imagined of soft and lovely in woman, soft and lovely, yet wild, so that, while you gazed with delight, you feared. Her low brow, though its fairness were tarnished by the sun, still gleamed beneath her raven-black hair; her eyes, which had reassumed some of their ancient gentleness, slept as it were beneath their heavy lids. Her angry look, which was lightning, her smile, which was as paradise, all elevated her above her fellow creatures; she seemed like the incarnation of some strange planetary spirit, that, robed in flesh, felt uneasy in its bonds, and longed to be away on the wings of its own will.

She spoke with trepidation: "Do not blush, my friend, or endeavour to conceal that paper; I know what it is; and, if you care for my peace of mind, if you love me, if the welfare of my almost lost soul be dear to you, let me see that writing."

"There is no consolation for you in it," replied Euthanasia, sadly.

"Nay, of that I alone can judge; look, I kneel to you, Euthanasia; and do you deny me? I intreat you to give me that paper."

"My own Beatrice, do not torture me thus: if I do not shew it you— Never mind: here it is; read it, and know what Castruccio is."

Beatrice read it with a peaceful air; and then, folding it up, said composedly;—"I see no ill in this; and his will shall be done. It is a strange coincidence, that I had already decided on what he advises; and I trust he will be glad to find that the wandering prophetess again seeks her antient path of religion and peace. I must explain these things to you, my Euthanasia. I know that you wish to remove to Florence: I can never leave this town. I shall never see him again, hear him speak, or be any thing to him; but to live within the same walls, to breathe the air of heaven which perhaps has hovered near him, this is a joy which I will never, never forego. My resolution is fixed: but you perish here; and would find loving and cherished friends there, where he can never come. I would not detain you; I have chosen the mode of my future destiny, and planned it all. The convent nearest to his palace is one of nuns dedicated to San Michele. I have already sent for the confessor of that convent; through him I shall make my peace with the church; and, when he believes me sufficiently pure to become an inhabitant of those sainted walls, I shall enter myself as a novice, and afterwards become a nun of that order. I intreat you, dearest, to stay only till my vows are made, when, wholly dedicated to heaven, I shall feel less an earthly separation."

She spoke in a hurried, faltering voice, and closed her speech in tears; she threw herself into Euthanasia's arms, and they both wept.—"Oh! no, unhappy, but dear, dear Beatrice, indeed you shall not leave me. I can be of little use now in the world to myself or others: but to cheer you, to teach you, as well as my poor skill will permit, the softest path to heaven, these shall be my tasks; you shall never leave me."

Beatrice disengaged herself from the arms of Euthanasia; and, casting up her eyes, with that look of inspiration which seemed to seek and find converse with the powers above, she said: "I thank you from the depth of my heart, and may God bless you as you deserve, divine Euthanasia; but I am fixed. Alas! my mind is as the waters, now lashed into waves by the winds of circumstance, now coldly dark under a lowering heaven, but never smiled upon by the life-giving sun. And this perishable frame is to my soul as a weak, tempest-beaten promontory, against which the Libeccio impels the undermining sea. I shall soon perish: but let my death be that of the holy; and that can alone be in the solitude of a cloister: that is the consummation of my fate. Oppose me no more: has not he pronounced? And I will obey his word, as if he were my king, my lord, my——Speak not; contradict me not; you see what a fragile being I am."

And now this Beatrice, this Paterin, who had so lately with heartfelt hatred told the tale of all the miseries that are suffered under the sun, and cursed the author of them, became as docile to the voice of the priest, as a seven-years-old child. The confessor for whom she had sent, found it no difficult task to turn her mind to the reception of his tenets; and prayer and penitence became again for her the law of the day. She never went out; she remained secluded in Euthanasia's palace; and, with her beads in her hand, her wild eyes turned heavenwards, she sought for peace, and she found at least a respite from some of the dreadful feelings that had hitherto tormented her.

In the mean time "the mother of the months" had many times waned, and again refilled her horn; and summer, and its treasure of blue skies, odorous flowers, merry insects, and sweet-voiced birds, again bade the world be happy. The peasant prepared the threshing floor, choosing a sunny spot which he carefully cleared of grass and weeds, and pouring water on it, beat it, till it was as hard as a barn-floor in the north. The ploughs, whose rough workmanship Virgil describes, lay useless beside the tilth, now filled with the rising corn: the primroses had faded; but one began to scent the myrtle on the mountains; the innumerable fireflies, loving the green wheat, made a second heaven of twinkling stars upon a verdant floor, or, darting among the olive copses, formed a fairy scene of the sweet Italian night; the soft-eyed oxen reposed in their stalls; and the flowers of the chesnuts and olives had given place to the young, half-formed fruit. This is the season that man has ever chosen for the destruction of his fellow-creatures, to make the brooks run blood, the air, filled with the carolling of happy birds, to echo also to the groans and shrieks of the dying, and the blue and serene heaven to become tainted with the dew which the unburied corpse exhales; winter were Bellona's fitting mate; but, no; she hangs about the neck of summer, who would fain shake her off, as might well be expected for so quarrelsome a bride.

Castruccio now possessed the whole territory of Lucca and several other circumjacent provinces, in peace and obedience. But his eyes were always turned towards Florence; and his most ardent wish was to humble, if not possess himself of, that city. He made another step towards it during the summer. The abbot of Pacciana got by popular favour entire power in Pistoia; he used this in behalf of Castruccio, turning out the Florentine ambassadors, and giving up to the prince of Lucca many of the strong-holds and towers of the Pistoian territory. Castruccio was possessed of the fortresses placed on the mountain which overlooked the town, where he hovered, like a hawk over his prey, ready to pounce, delaying only for the destined minute.

During this summer also he conceived some hopes of taking Pisa. The head of the government there, who reigned entirely through the affections of the people, suddenly offended his masters; he was decapitated; and the various parties in the town, running to arms, entered into a bloody warfare. At this moment Castruccio appeared with his army on the hill of St. Giuliano: this sight pacified the combatants; they elected a new lord, and turned their powers towards resisting the common enemy. Castruccio retreated to Lucca; but he was so moved by the overthrow of the Pisan chief, that, resolving to trust no more, as he had hitherto done, to the affections of his people, he erected in the same year a strong fortress within the walls of his city, which he called Agosta. He spared no expence or labour in it; and it was considered by all as the most magnificent work of those days: it was situated in that part of the town which looks towards Pisa, surrounded by a strong and high wall, and fortified by thirty towers. The inhabitants of a whole quarter were turned out of their dwellings, to make room for this new symbol of tyranny; and here he, his family, and followers, lived in proud security.

Towards the end of the month of June, Euthanasia, who had hitherto been occupied in attending to the sorrows of Beatrice, received information, that one of her most valued Florentine friends was dangerously ill, and earnestly desired her attendance. She mentioned this to her guest; and Beatrice, ever variable, was then in a docile mood. She had long listened with deep and earnest faith to the lessons of Padre Lanfranco, the confessor of the convent to which she was about to retire. It would seem that this old man humoured warily and wisely her disturbed understanding; for she appeared at peace with herself and others: if she now wept, she did not accuse, as she had before done, Him who had created the fountain of her tears.

"Go, kind friend," said she to Euthanasia; "go; but return again. Remember, I claim your companionship, until I take the veil,—then you are free. Methinks, I should like to be left now in utter solitude, I could commune more intensely with the hopes and heavenly gifts that I entertain. Go; blessed spirit of Good, guardian Angel of poor Beatrice, poor in all but gratitude,—you shall not see your work marred on your return; you will still find me the good, obedient child, which I have been, now, I think, for more than a month."

Euthanasia left her with pain, and with a mournful presentiment; but, as all wore the aspect of peace, she thought herself bound to obey the voice of friendship, and to see, perhaps for the last time, one who had been the friend and companion of her early youth; and she departed for Florence. There were for her too many associations allied to the Val di Nievole, to permit her to choose that route. Besides Castruccio's army occupied the passes, and she feared to meet him. She accordingly went round by Pisa. Nothing could be more beautiful than the country; the low Pisan hills covered with chesnut and olive woods, interspersed with darker patches of pine and cork (while, among all, the cypresses raised their tapering spires), and, crowned by castles and towers, bounded in a plain of unparalleled fertility. The corn was cutting, and the song of the reapers kept time as it were with the noisy cicale in the olive trees, and the chirping birds. Peace, for the first time for several years, sat brooding with outspread wings over the land; and underneath their blessed shade sprung joy and plenty.

Euthanasia arrived at Florence. She found her friend recovered; but all her acquaintance, who had eagerly expected her arrival, were much disappointed when they heard that it was her intention to return to Lucca. She however both loved and pitied Beatrice too much, to be wanting in any of the duties of friendship towards her. After a month's residence in her natal and beloved city, she again departed from Florence. In the mean time what had become of the ill-fated prophetess?

CHAPTER VI

The Albinois Bindo had been greatly struck by the appearance of Beatrice. There was a wildness in her countenance and gestures that excited his curiosity; and he seemed to feel instinctively that she had about her the marks of one who dealt with unembodied spirits. He had ventured to speak to his mistress concerning her; but he learnt nothing except that Ferrara was her native town. With this slight information he visited his friend, the witch, and they canvassed the subject together.

"Her eye sees beyond this world," said Bindo; "if you were to look on her, you would find a companion in your art. I have discovered that there is a mysterious connexion between her and the prince: he liberated her when she was imprisoned by the Dominican fathers, as a Paterin, they say, but I suspect that it was for magic."

"At any rate," replied the witch, "there is a mystery in this that I will clear up. I will go to Ferrara, and learn who and what she is. Expect me back in less than a month; in the mean time watch her; watch every word and action; something may come of this."

The witch went to Ferrara. She traversed the hills, and went by unknown paths, and across the untrodden mountains, guided either by her former experience, or by the arch fiend himself; for it required almost supernatural knowledge to trace her way among the heaped and confused range of the Apennines. She walked at night, and rested during the day, and saw the sun many times rise and set among the wild forests that covered the hills. At Ferrara she learnt what she desired: Beatrice, the *Ancilla Dei*, the prophetess, was not forgotten; even her connexion with Castruccio had been guessed at; and some even dared assert, that she had never quitted Lucca, or the palace of the prince, during her pretended pilgrimage to Rome. The witch returned, joyful to think that she had now obtained an instrument for some of her projects.

What were her projects? They had not that settled aim and undeviating course which one object might inspire. Her desire was malice; and her present hope, to impress upon Bindo some notion of the powers to which she pretended. She had been young once; and her nature, never mild, had been turned to ferocity by wrongs which had been received so long ago, that the authors of them were all dead, and she, the victim, alone survived. Calumny had blasted her name; her dearest affections had been blighted; her children torn from her; and she remained to execrate and to avenge.

Her evil propensities had long exhausted themselves in acts of petty mischief among the peasantry; but her connexion with Bindo gave her hopes of a wider scope for wickedness. To injure Castruccio, or to benefit Euthanasia, was alike indifferent to her. She saw and understood more of the human heart than Bindo did: she knew, that Euthanasia had once loved the prince; and injury to him she hoped would carry a double sting. She was old, perhaps about to die; and she thought that there would be a pleasure in expiring amidst the groans of the victims of her malice.

In these days, when the passions, if they are not milder, are more restrained, and assume a more conventional appearance, it will be doubted if such fiendish love of mischief ever existed; but that it did, all tradition and history prove. It was believed, that the witch loved evil as her daily bread, and that she had sold her soul to the devil to do ill alone; *she* knew how powerless she was; but she desired to fill in every part the character attributed to her.

As she returned over the Apennines, she planned her future conduct; she thought she saw one mighty ruin envelop three master-spirits of the human kind, plotted by her alone. It was a dangerous experiment. "But I must die," she cried; "and what death will be sweeter, even if it be in the midst of flames, if so many share the torments with me? And thou, puny abortion, who darest with trembling hands meddle in work beyond thee, thou also shalt taste the poison so long withheld! A canker cling to you all! I have long sought for labour suited to my genius; and now I have found it."

It was on the day previous to the departure of Euthanasia for Florence, that the witch returned: she met Bindo with a ghastly smile. "All," she cried, "is as you wish; the star of Castruccio will be extinguished behind the murky cloud which this same Beatrice will raise. Bring her to me; in time you shall know all: but be wary; the countess must be blind and deaf to our machinations."

Euthanasia had departed, leaving Beatrice far calmer than she had before been since her release from prison. But no feelings were more fluctuating than those of the poor prophetess. The day after she had parted from her protectress, Padre Lanfranco had been called upon urgent business to Sienna; and she was left without a guide to the workings of her own mind. She could not stand this; the consolations of Euthanasia, and the exhortations of the priest were alike forgotten; and Beatrice, turned out, as it were, without shelter, fell into repinings and despair.

She had ardently desired to see Castruccio; but her confessor had commanded her to avoid all occasions of meeting him, if she wished to fit herself for the holy life to which she said she felt herself called. Beatrice was easily led; but she had no command over herself; and, the moment she was left to her own guidance, she was hurried away by the slightest impression.

Castruccio had just returned from Pistoia on the news of the insurrection of Pisa; and it was said that he would again quit Lucca on the following morning. "Now or never," thought Beatrice, "I may have my will unreproved; if this day escape, I am again surrounded, enchained; I might see him, hear his voice; oh! that I had courage to make the attempt! Yet I fear that this may be the suggestion of some evil spirit; I must not, dare not see him."

She wept and prayed; but in vain. In her days of extatic reverie she had sanctified and obeyed every impulse as of divine origin; and now she could not withstand the impressions she felt. She wrapped a coarse capuchin around her, and sallied forth, with trembling steps, and eyes gleaming with tears, to go and gaze on the form of him for whom she had sacrificed her all. Hardly had she proceeded two paces from Euthanasia's palace-gate, before a form—a man—passed before her, and with a loud shriek she fell senseless on the pavement. She was brought back to the house, and carefully nursed; but several days elapsed, while, still possessed with fever, she raved of the most tremendous and appalling scenes and actions, which she fancied were taking place around her. The man whom she had seen was Tripalda; and from what she said in her delirium, it might be gathered, that he had been an actor in the frightful wrongs she had endured during her strange imprisonment in the Campagna di Roma. She was attended on with kindness, and she recovered; and such was the effect of her delirium, that she persuaded herself that what had so terrified her, was a mere vision conjured up by her imagination. She thought that the vivid image of this partner of her enemy's crimes, thus coming across her while she was on the point of disobeying her confessor's injunction, was a warning and punishment from heaven.

Euthanasia was away, and Beatrice dared not speak to any: she brooded in her own mind over the appearance, mysterious as she thought it, of this man; until her fancy was so high wrought, that she feared her very shadow on the wall; and the echo of her own steps as she trod the marble pavement of her chamber, made her tremble with terror; the scenes she had witnessed, the horrors that she had endured in that unhallowed asylum of crime, presented themselves to her in their most vivid colours; she remembered all, saw all; and the deep anguish she felt was no longer mitigated by converse with her friend.

"Oh, cruel, unkind Euthanasia!" she cried, "why did you leave me? My only hope, my only trust was in you; and you desert me. Alas! alas! I am a broken reed, and none will support me; the winds blow, and I am prostrated to the ground; and, if I rise again, I am bruised, almost annihilated.

"Oh! that I could die! and yet I fear death. Oh! thou, who wert my teacher and saviour, thou who expiredst smiling amidst flames, would that thou wert here to teach me to die! What do I in this fair garden of the world? I am a weed, a noxious insect; would that some superior power would root me out utterly, or some giant-foot tread me to dust! Yet I ask for what I do not wish. Was he a good God that moulded all the agonizing contradictions of this frail heart?

"Yet hush, presumptuous spirit! recall no more those lessons, which I hoped had been forgotten. Father! God! behold the most miserable and weakest of thy creatures; teach me to die; and then kill me!"

She sat in the neglected garden of the palace, on one of the pedestals which had been placed as a stand for the pots containing lemon-trees; she leaned her head upon her hand, while the tears trickled down unheeded. It had been her delight, ever since her arrival at Lucca, to rove in this wild garden; and sometimes, when the sun had been long set, and the sound of the *Ave Maria* had died away, she would sit there, and, fixing her eyes on the brightest star of the heavens, would sing the remembered melodies of her childhood. Nothing recalls past feeling so strongly as the notes of once-loved music; the memory was almost too much for her; and her eyes streamed tears, as she sang the sweetest lay that mortal ear had ever heard. Euthanasia had listened, she loved to listen, to her wild airs; and, as Beatrice saw her own deep emotions reflected in the beaming eyes of her friend, she felt soothed. But she was now alone; she felt the solitude; she felt, that she sang, and that none heeded her song: but, as the violet breathes as sweet an odour on the indifferent air, as when the loveliest creature in the world bends over it to inhale its fragrance; so did Beatrice now sing in solitude, while, her heart warmed, her imagination expanded, and she felt a transport which was pleasure, although a sea of black despair was its near boundary.

As she sang, Bindo came near her unperceived. He had never addressed her before; and she had never observed him: she was one of those persons, who feel their own life and identity so much, that they seem to have no spare feeling and sense for the uninteresting events and persons that pass around them. He now spoke in a loud voice, arousing her from her deep reverie:

"Awake, prophetess; it is not well that you should sleep; the spirits of the air have work for you; all Tuscany feels your super-human presence."

Beatrice started, and gazed with surprize on the being who thus addressed her: his dwarfish stature, his white hair and eyelashes, his pale and wrinkled face, and his light reddish eyes gave him a strange appearance; he looked indeed like one of the spirits whose existence he asserted; and she shuddered as she beheld him.

"I come," continued Bindo, "from one, whose eye can see the forms that pass, to me viewless, through the air; from one, who has thunder and tempest like dogs in a leash, and who can wind and unwind the will of man, as the simple girl spins thread from her distaff. I bear a message to you."

"Of whom do you speak? I do not understand you."

"You will understand her words; for between the gifted there are signs, which none else know, but which bind them fast together."

"Are you one of those?" asked the wondering girl.

"I am not," replied Bindo; "you know that I am not, though I did not tell you. Are you not Beatrice, the prophetess of Ferrara? But my words are weak. There is one who lives in a cavern not far off, who was called, when young, Fior di Ligi, and now she calls herself Fior di Mandragola; she rules the spirits who live about us, and is powerful over the seasons, and over the misfortunes and sorrows of life. She bade me tell you to awake; this night I will lead you to her; and she will by her incantations take off the veil which spirits of darkness have thrown over you."

"You talk of nothing; who are you?"

"I am a servant of the countess of Valperga; nothing more; a poor, ignorant, despised dwarf, a blight, a stunt: but I am more powerful in my weakness, than they with their giant limbs and strong muscles;—at least I have that strength, as long as I am obedient to her of whom I spoke. These are the words she bade me say to you,—'There is a cloud over you which words of power can dispel; you are that which you seemed, and not that which you believe';—come to the cavern of Fior di Mandragola; and she will restore you to that height, from which the ignorance of others, and your own want of faith have precipitated you."

"And who is Fior di Mandragola?"

"A witch,—a woman with grey hair and decrepid limbs; she is clothed in rags, and feeds upon acorns and wood-nuts; but she is greater than any queen. If she were to command, this blue sky would be covered with clouds, the Serchio would overflow, and the plain of Lucca heave with earthquake; she makes men fear they know not what; for by her command spirits tug them by the hair, and they shiver with dread. One only she cannot command;

one will, one fortune, one power cannot be controled by her; but your star surmounts his.—So, come, that you may know how to rule him."

"Whom?"

"The prince of Lucca."

"Away! you know not what you say."

"I obey; speak not of this to the countess; I will be at your chamber-window by midnight."

Bindo retreated, leaving Beatrice startled and trembling. She did not rely on his wild creed; but she felt as if it might be true. She had once believed in the command of man over supernatural agency; and she had thrown aside that creed, when she lost her faith in her own powers. She ran rapidly in her thoughts over all that had occurred to her of this nature, her extacies, her delirious and joyous aspirations,—they were more dead and cold, than the white ashes of a long-extinguished fire;—but other events had occurred, and she had felt inexplicable emotions which seemed to link her to other existences. She remembered her dream; and, covering her eyes with her hands, she endeavoured to recal what words and forms had been revealed to her on that occasion——vainly; the attempt served only more to shake a reason already tottering. It awoke her however from her unbelief; and she again felt those deep and inquisitive thoughts, that had for many years been the life of her being. She resolved to visit Fior di Mandragola; she knew not why, but curiosity was mingled with the desire of change and freedom; she thought that it would be delightful to visit at midnight the witch's cave, guided by the strange Albinois. Beatrice was left alone to her own reflections for the whole evening; they were ever dreadful, except when the vivacity of her imagination mingled rainbows with the tempest.

Night came; and, wrapping a capuchin around her, she mounted the horse that Bindo had brought, and followed him across the country, towards the mountains which divide the Lucchese from the Modenese territory; the dark forests extended into the valley, contrasting their black shadows with the dun hues of the low country; the stars shone keenly above. They rode swiftly; but the way was long; and it was two o'clock before they arrived at the witch's cave. It was a dreary habitation: and now, as the shades of night fell upon it, it appeared more desolate than ever; the pines made a sorrowful singing above it; the earth around was herbless; and a few pine cones lay about, mingled with the grey rock that here and there peeped above the soil.

The witch sat at the door of the hovel. She was a strange being: her person was short, almost deformed, shrivelled and dried up, but agile and swift of motion; her brown and leathern face was drawn into a thousand lines; and the flesh of her cheeks, thus deformed, seemed hardly human; her hands were large, bony, and thin; she was unlike every other animal, but also was she unlike humanity, and seemed to form a species apart, which might well inspire the country people with awe. When she saw Beatrice, she arose, and advanced towards her, saying, "What do you here, child of a sleeping power? Come you here to teach, or to learn the secrets of our art?"

"I come at your own request," replied Beatrice, haughtily; "if you have nothing to say to me, I return."

"I have much to say to you," said Mandragola; "for I would awaken a spirit from lethargy, that can command us all. You are the mistress of those, of whom I am the slave; will it, and a thousand spirits wait your bidding; look, like subdued hounds they now crouch at your feet, knowing that you are their superior. It is my glory to *obey* them,—how far do *you* transcend me!"

"You talk in riddles, good mother; I see no spirits, I feel no power."

"And if you did, would you be here? Here, at the cavern of a poor witch, who, spelling her incantations, and doing such penance as would make your young blood freeze but to hear it, just earns a power hardly gained, quickly to be resigned. But you could ride the winds, command the vegetation of the earth, and have all mankind your slaves. I ask you whether you did not once feel that strength? For a moment you were eclipsed; but the influence of the evil planet is well nigh gone, and you may now rule all,—will you accept this dominion?"

"Your words appear idle to me; give them proof, and I will listen."

"Consult your own heart, prophetess; and that will teach you far more than I can. Does it not contain strange secrets known only to yourself? Have you never owned a power, which dwelt within you, and you felt your own mind distinct from it, as if it were more wise than you; so wise that you confessed, but could not comprehend its wisdom? Has it not revealed to you that, which without its aid you never could have known? Have you not seen this other self?"

"Stop, wonderful woman, if you would not madden me," screamed the poor terrified Beatrice. "That is the key, the unbreakable link of my existence; that dream must either place me above humanity, or destroy me."

"You own this power?" cried the witch triumphantly.

"Send away the Albinois, and I will tell you all. [At the beck of the witch Bindo withdrew.] Yet I gasp for breath, and fear possesses me. What do you tell me of power? I feel that I am ruled; and, when this dream comes over me, as it now does, I am no longer myself. I dreamed of a flood, of a waste of white, still waters, of mountains, of a real scene which I had never beheld. There was a vast, black house standing in the midst of the water; a concourse of dark shapes hovered about me; and suddenly I was transported into a boat which was to convey me to that mansion. Strange! another boat like to mine moved beside us; its prow was carved in the same manner; its rowers, the same in number, the same in habiliment, struck the water with their oars at the same time with ours; a woman sate near the stern, aghast and wild as I;—but their boat cut the waves without sound, their oars splashed not the waters as they struck them, and, though the boats were alike black, yet not like mine did this other cast a black shadow on the water. We landed together; I could not walk for fear; I was carried into a large room, and left alone; I leaned against the hangings, and there advanced to meet me another form. It was myself; I knew it; it stood before me, melancholy and silent; the very air about it was still. I can tell no more;—a few minutes ago I remembered nothing of all this; a few moments, and I distinctly remembered the words it spoke; they have now faded. Yes; there is something mysterious in my nature, which I cannot fathom."

Beatrice shivered; her face was deadly pale, and her eyes were glazed by fear. The witch had now tuned her instrument, and she proceeded to play on it with a master's hand.

"Heavenly girl," she said, "I acknowledge myself your slave. Command me and my powers, as you will; they will do all you bid them;—but that is little. There are other spirits, which belong not to the elements, but to the mind and fortunes of man, over which I have no sway, but which are attendant upon you. Fear not! The revelations you have received are almost too tremendous for your weak human frame; but gather strength; for your body and your spirit may master all the kings of the earth. That other self, which at one time lives within you, and anon wanders at will over the boundless universe, is a pure and immediate emanation of the divinity, and, as such, commands all creatures, be they earthly or ethereal. As yet you have seen it only in a dream; have faith, and the consciousness of its presence will visit your waking reveries."

Beatrice sighed deeply, and said: "I was in hope that my part was done, and that I should die without more agitation and fear; but I am marked, and cannot combat with my destiny. Strange as is the tale which I have just related, I cannot believe what you say: and, though doubtless there are other existences, of which we know nothing, yet I do not believe that we can have communication with, and far less power over them. I would fain preserve the little reason I have still left me; and that tells me that what you say is false."

"But if I can prove it to be true?"

"How?"

"Ask what you will! Would you see the cloudless sky become black and tempestuous? Would you hear the roaring of the overflowing waters, or see the animals of the forest congregate at my feet? Or, would you exert your own power? Would you draw towards you by your powerful incantations, one whom you wish to see, and who must obey your call? If you speak, all must obey; the prince himself, the victorious Castruccio, could not resist you."

The burning cheeks, and flashing eyes of the prophetess, shewed the agitation that this proposal excited in her heart. Poor girl! she still loved; that wound still festered, ever unhealed. She would have risked her soul, to gain a moment's power over Castruccio. She paused; and then said, "In three days I will tell you what I wish, and what I will do."

"In the mean time swear never to reveal this visit, this cavern, or my name: swear by yourself."

"A foolish vow,—by myself I swear."

"Enough; you dare not break that oath."

The witch retreated into her cave; and Bindo came forward to conduct Beatrice home. She was faint and tired; and day dawned before they arrived at the palace of Euthanasia.

The three following days were days of doubt and trepidation for the unfortunate Beatrice. At one moment she utterly discredited the pretensions of Mandragola; but then her imagination, that evil pilot for her, suggested, *Yet, if it should be so!* and then she would picture forth the scenes she desired, until she gasped with expectation. At last, she thought,—"There will be no harm in the experiment; if her promises are vain, no injury will result;—if true—To be sure I know they are not; but something will happen, and at least I will try.

"I know that Euthanasia, and more than she, Padre Lanfranco, would tell me, that, if true, this woman deals with the devil, and that I, who have lately saved my soul from his grasp, should beware of trusting myself within his reach. All this is well to children and old women; but I have already tempted the powers above me too far to flinch now. Am I not, was I not, a Paterin? Euthanasia, who has never wandered from the straight line of her duty, and Lanfranco, who has learned his morality in a cloister, cannot know what it most becomes an excommunicated wretch like me to do.

"Yet I am very ungrateful and wicked, when I say this; ungrateful to their prayers, wicked in transgressing the laws which God has promulgated.

"What does this woman say? that I shall see him, that he will obey my voice, and that, not by magic art, but by that innate power, which, by the order of the universe, one spirit possesses over another:—that I shall see him, as I have seen him!—Oh, saints of heaven, suffer me not to be tempted thus! But no,—the heavenly powers deign not to interfere; they know my weakness, my incapacity to resist,—but, like most careless guardians, they permit that to approach which must overcome me. I am resolved; she shall guide me; if nothing come (as most surely nothing will come), it imports not. And, if I am destined for one moment more in this most wretched life to taste of joy, others may (but I will not) dash the intoxicating draught away."

She thought thus, and spoke thus to her secret mind; but every hour her resolution fluctuated, and remorse, hope, and dread possessed her by turns. She feared to be alone; but the presence of an indifferent person made her nerves tremble with the restraint she was obliged to keep upon herself. There seemed some link of confidence between her and Bindo; and she called for him to dispel the appalling sensations with which solitude inspired her. He came; and his conversation only tended to increase her chaos of conflicting thoughts. He related the wonderful exploits of Mandragola; how he had seen her call lightning and cloud from the south, and how at her bidding the soft western wind would suddenly arise, and dispel the wondrous tempests she had brewed; how the planet of night obeyed her, and that, once during the full moon, this planet had suddenly deserted the sky, but that, while the heavens were blank and rayless, its image continued to lie placidly in the stream near which they stood. He related the strange effects she had produced upon the minds of men, forcing them most unwillingly to do her pleasure; at other times depriving them of their senses, so that for many hours they wandered about like madmen, until at her command their faculties were restored to them.

Beatrice listened, half in disdain, half in fear; her conclusion still was,—"The experiment is worth trying; if her words be false, there is no harm done; if true"—and then her imagination pictured forth happiness that never should be hers.

CHAPTER VII

On the third night she returned to the witch. "You need not speak," said Mandragola, "I know your thoughts; you hardly believe my words, yet you are determined to make the trial. It is well; I should be surer of success, if you had implicit faith in my powers and your own; but it is enough. What do you wish to effect?"

"First, mother, I must know what I can do."

"Your power is almost illimitable; but that of which I spoke, and that power which you prize most, is the power which you possess over the prince of Lucca. Do you wish to see him? Do you wish in solitude, with none but me near, to see him come, to hear him renew his antient vows?"

"He never made vows to me," cried Beatrice angrily; "he was bound to me, I thought, by stronger ties than mortal oaths; that is past for ever; but, except the salvation of my soul, I would sacrifice every thing to see him once again, divested of the ceremonial of power, listening to what will never be told, consoling her who can never be consoled."

"That is easy work," said the witch, with alacrity; "but first swear, swear by all that you hold sacred in the world, by your life, by his, that you will never disclose this conversation, or what I shall now reveal to you, or hint in any manner the work we shall undertake."

Beatrice shivered; she could no longer stand, she sunk to the ground: the witch went into the hut, and brought her a bowl of water; Beatrice put it to her lips; then suddenly withdrawing it, she cried,—"You have given me a poisonous drug, either to kill me, or undermine my understanding;—dare you thus trifle with me?"

The witch took the bowl from her hand, and drank the liquid it contained: "Take shame for your mistrust," she said; "this was pure water from the spring; and, except that the charmed moon-beams sleep on it, even when you see not the moon in the sky, it does not differ from the waters of any other fountain. Now speak; do you swear secrecy?"

Again the prophetess paused. But curiosity and hope hurried her beyond discretion; and with folded hands placed between the dry and skinny palms of the witch, she pronounced the vow that was dictated.

Mandragola then said: "This satisfies me. The moon is now on the wane: when she fills again, I will send Bindo to inform you what is to be done. Fear not, but that all will be well."

Beatrice returned to Lucca. Her glazed eyes and pale cheeks told that the spirit which animated her now found nor rest nor hope. She dreaded to look forward to the fearful trial she was about to make; and yet she could think of nothing else. Her rosary was thrown aside; her prayers were forgotten; and love again reassumed his throne in her heart. Her reason was disturbed by doubt and fear; and she often sat whole hours, her eye fixed upon the earth, her parted lips pale, her hands closed with convulsive strength, as she tried to reason herself into disbelief concerning the promises and assertions of Mandragola. It was too much for her weak frame; if the witch had been near her to mark the wasting of her faculties, she might have wound her plot so as to inspire her with some courage: but no one was near except Bindo; and he by his tales, and his own fears and belief, only increased the combat of feelings to which the prophetess was a prey.

Euthanasia returned from Florence. She was much disappointed, much grieved, to find her friend far worse both in body and mind, than when she left her. More than all wildness of words and manner, she feared her silence and reserve, so very unlike her latest disposition. If the convent, or her future plans were named, she listened calmly, but did not reply; no intreaties could persuade her to give words to that which preyed upon her mind. She would weep; and then, flying from the affectionate reproaches of her protectress, she would shut herself up to grieve alone, or far more dangerously to dream of the return of love and joy. Euthanasia reasoned, persuaded, intreated, but vainly: accustomed to the caprices of this unfortunate girl, she saw nothing in what now occurred, that appeared to arise from any external impulse; and she hoped that indulgence and kindness would in time restore her to her former calm. She reproached herself for having left her; and she resolved that, unless indeed Beatrice took the veil, which now seemed doubtful, she would never again separate herself from her. She loved her tenderly, and pitied her so truly, that she was willing to sacrifice all her own hopes of future peace to soothe and restore her to some degree of happiness.

Her endeavours were useless. The melancholy of poor Beatrice was undissipated by the slightest gleam of tranquillity: for five days she had not spoken, and had hardly touched any food. Euthanasia tried in vain to console her, and, hopeless of good, sought to excite any passion that might rouse her from her mute reveries; she spoke not, but wandered restlessly from room to room, or among the wild paths of the garden; and thence she would have escaped into the open country, but that her weak limbs sunk beneath her. One night Euthanasia slept, when Beatrice suddenly entered the room; and, twining herself round her neck, and wrapping the long and thick hair of her friend around her brows— —

"Save me!" she cried, "save me from madness, which, as a fiend, pursues and haunts me. I endeavour to fly him; but still he hovers near: is there no escape? Oh! if God be good, surely he will redeem my soul from this curse. I would fain preserve my reason; my lips are bloodless, and my hair quite grey; I am a skeleton without flesh or form; I am to what lives, like the waning moon at noonday, which floats up as a vapour, and the blue air seems to penetrate its pale and sickly form. Happiness, beauty, love have passed away; but I would fain preserve that without which I am as a poor hunted beast, whose sole repose is on the spear of the huntsman. Breathe on me, Euthanasia, breathe on my hands, my eyes; perhaps some portion of calm may flow from your bosom to mine. I only wish not to be mad; yet, if what is said be true, these wonderful things may be, and I still sane. There, there, your hand is cool; press my head. I know you well; you are Euthanasia; I am Beatrice; I may still be preserved from madness."

Euthanasia wept; she folded Beatrice in her arms; she placed her cool hand on her brow, and her pale cheek close to the flushed one of the poor sick girl. Beatrice rested a few moments in silence; and then again she spoke. "It has been said, that I am a witch, one who has power over the elements, and still more over the mind of man. I do not believe this: once, I know, a very long time ago, I fancied myself a prophetess; but I awoke from that dream many years since. Why then do they madden me with these insinuations? I will tell you, Euthanasia (sweet name, dear, much-loved friend), that sometimes I fancy this is true.—Oh! that I could tell the heavy secret that weighs upon my soul! I have sworn—they did not well, that made me swear:—yet there is some truth in what they say, doubtless there is some truth, and it shall be *proved*. Well, well; I have sworn, and I will not tell—Good night, dearest; I shall sleep now; so not a word more; I have reasoned with myself, and am content."

Beatrice crept back to her chamber; but Euthanasia could not again rest. She was amazed at her friend's strange words, and tried to divine whether they proceeded from the heated imagination of the prophetess, or from some real event of which Euthanasia was ignorant; but she had no clue to guide her in her conjectures; and it appeared to her most probable, that Beatrice was moved by the suggestions of her own heart; she could not guess the dreadful and maniac thoughts that really disturbed her, or the frightful incitements that had been employed to deceive her.

A fortnight passed thus; when the Albinois brought a message from Mandragola, bidding Beatrice repair that same night at twelve, to a wood about four miles from Lucca. At this time Castruccio was employed in building the tower of Nozzano, on a small hill which was surrounded by the wood chosen by the witch. The weather (it was in the month of July) was exceedingly hot; the cattle panted beneath the sun; the earth was herbless; all life decayed: but delicious nights succeeded these oppressive days; and Castruccio was accustomed to repair, as early as two in the morning, to visit the fortress. Mandragola knew the spot near which he passed; and she so planned her scheme, that her incantation should be wound to the desired pitch, at the moment when he should ride through the wood: and thus, to the simple mind of the Albinois, and the exalted imagination of Beatrice, afford a proof of the extent of her power.

It is impossible to say what her object was in all this; she might be merely instigated by the desire to excite respect and terror, and have trusted that this apparent confirmation of her assertions would enable her to acquire unlimited power over the mind of her victims. She did not intend on this occasion that Beatrice should speak to the prince;—that she should call for him, and he appear, was sufficient mummery for one day: another time more might be done, and another step taken in the labyrinth of error and fraud.

That same night Bindo tapped at the door of Beatrice's chamber. The prophetess opened it;—she looked aghast and wild, but spoke not.—"This is the hour," said the Albinois.

"Wrap your cloak round you," he continued, "that you may not be known." Beatrice did as he desired, moving her arms like inanimate machines, and turning her eyes around, as if she saw nothing. Bindo led her down-stairs; they quitted the palace by a small back door; he made her mount a horse; and they rode out of the town. All passed in silence; Beatrice hardly appeared to know whither she was going, or why she went; the bridle fell from her hands, and hung loosely on the horse's neck; but the animal mechanically followed Bindo's horse, which led the way.

They arrived at the wood, and dismounted. Bindo tied the horses to a tree, and proceeded cautiously through the intricate paths of the forest. It was an ilex wood; and the dark foliage canopied them above, while the moon-beams penetrated through the interstices of the leaves, and made a chequered shadow upon the ground, which was despoiled of its grassy covering through long drouth. At length they came to a more trodden road; and this led to a kind of woody amphitheatre, an open space in the midst of the trees, one of the corners of which the path traversed, and all around the ilexes formed a circular boundary of ample circumference. At one of the extremities, farthest from the path, was a fountain, which kept a soft murmuring all the still night through. Near this fountain the witch sat: she was weaving two coronals of ivy, and muttering as she wove; Beatrice and the Albinois were before her, but she appeared not to notice them. Beatrice stood, her arms hanging down, her head fallen on her bosom in a mute lethargy, her cloak had dropt from her shoulders, and fallen to her feet; she was dressed, as the witch had commanded, in white: several years had passed since she had been thus habited, and her attire displayed the thinness of her form and the paleness of her wasted cheeks; her hands were skinny and yellow, her hair perfectly grey; a few weeks ago, although mingled with white, its antient colour was preserved; but since then it had quite changed; her eyes were sunken, ringed with black, and rayless.

When the witch had finished her work, she rose; and, taking some of the water of the fountain in the hollow of her hand, she threw it over Beatrice, and then crowned her with one of the chaplets; she placed the other on her own head; and then she said to Bindo:—"I am about to sanctify this place; you must depart."

Bindo bowed assent, and disappeared. She took up a curiously fashioned ewer of brass; and, filling it at the fount, she walked round the amphitheatre of trees, sprinkling the ground as she went, and muttering her incantations, till she came round again to the spot, where Beatrice stood, white, motionless, and silent. "You appear faint, daughter," she said; "drink of this water."—She put it to the lips of her victim, who drank it eagerly; and immediately a change took place in her appearance; her eyes lighted up, her cheeks were flushed, the heavy chain of mortality seemed to fall from her, she became active and even gay; by degrees a kind of transport seized her, a drunkenness of spirit, which made her lose all constraint over her words and actions, although it did not blind her to what was passing around. [2]

"Aye, mother," she said, "I know what I come for; now let us begin; I am an enchantress, you say; I can conjure him to appear, who before defied my powers? be it so;—let us begin."

"Listen," replied Mandragola, "no art requires so much patience as ours. We will make our incantations; and you will see him pass on horseback along that road: do not now seek to speak to him. Exercise your power moderately at first; and it will be greater afterwards: bind him now with a straw; in time he will be inextricably enthralled. To-night be it enough that you see him."

"Enough! oh! I would lay down my life for one, one moment's sight!"

The night was perfectly still; the air was sultry, and not a leaf moved: the trees, bathed as it were in the cold moonshine, slept; and the earth received their moveless shadows on her quiet bosom. The fountain murmured on;

beside it stood the witch and Beatrice;—Beatrice, her eyes lifted to heaven, her arms crossed on her bosom, her hair clinging round her faded neck. Mandragola was full of business; she piled a small heap of wood, walking often around it, singing or chanting strange verses, and scattering water and oil about her; she drew, with a wand formed of a peeled chesnut-bough, a circle which surrounded the pile and the spot whereon Beatrice stood, and commanded her not to pass the line till she should give permission; since that circle would preserve her from the spirits that their terrible incantations had called around them. She then turned to the pile again, and placed on it incense and odoriferous gums, and plants, and strange devices, cut in wood, or moulded in wax, which no one might understand: then to crown the work she cut off a lock of Beatrice's hair, and threw it on the heap.

She had just accomplished this work, when a slight sound struck her ear; "Now is the time!" she exclaimed; and she set up a wild song to drown the trampling of the approaching horses; she lighted a torch, and cried— "This is your work, mistress of the powers of air; light the pyre, and call thrice on the name of the prince of Lucca!"

Beatrice started forward with frantic haste; she seized the torch, thrust it into the pile, which caught the flame, and blazed up as she cried aloud, "Castruccio! Castruccio! Castruccio!"

And then, unable to restrain her impatience, she ran towards the path in which Mandragola had said he would appear. The witch called on her to stay; but she was too decrepid to follow swiftly to stop her: the sound of coming horsemen was now distinctly heard; Beatrice threw herself on her knees, in the midst of the path by which they must pass; with flashing eyes and outstretched arms, she gazed eagerly forwards: the dark wood covered her; the moon beams fell on her; and there she, once the loveliest, now the most lost, the most utterly undone of women, kneeled in frantic expectation. The horsemen approached; a turn in the path concealed them, until they were full upon her; and then she saw Castruccio and Tripalda advance. Her brain, already on fire with impatience, and her spirits exalted by the drug administered to her, could no longer sustain the sensations that overpowered her. The presence of Tripalda was to her the sign of diabolical interference; she believed him dead; that it was his spirit which then appeared; and, if so, it was also an unreal form, the resemblance of Castruccio alone, that she beheld.— —She sunk in convulsions on the road.

Castruccio, surprised at what he saw, leaped from his horse; and his example was followed by his attendants. The witch, who had hitherto hobbled towards Beatrice, seeing them dismount, endeavoured to escape; but Tripalda, who, judging of others by himself, was ever ready to suspect knavery, cut off her retreat, and ordered two of the servants to hold her. She submitted quietly, but remained invincibly silent to all the questions that were put to her. Beatrice was carried to the fountain; and they endeavoured, by chafing her temples, and rubbing her hands, to bring her to life: the prince himself supported her head; but he did not recognize her; so utterly was she changed from what the prophetess of Ferrara had been. Once she opened her eyes; she saw the face of Castruccio leaning over her, and she smiled. Castruccio thought that he knew that smile; but Tripalda, leaving the witch, pressed in among those who were about her.—No one who had seen him could ever forget him; she saw what she believed to be the evil genius of her life; and she again sunk into insensibility.

In the mean time the Albinois, who had been lurking near the spot, hearing the trampling of horses, and the sound of men's voices, ventured forward. Mandragola saw him first, as he came into the moonshine from under the dark covert of trees. She darted forward, and cried aloud—"Fly! fly!" Her words and gesture attracted the notice of her guards, as Bindo turned about to obey her orders. They pursued him, and easily took him prisoner.

He was brought to Castruccio, who instantly recognized him. "What do you here?" he demanded. "Are you not the servant of the countess of Valperga?"

"I am."

"Who then is this lady? and how came you here?"

"That is Beatrice of Ferrara. I can tell you no more until she" (pointing to the witch) "gives me leave."

The name of Beatrice was sufficient to transfix the prince with pity and remorse. "Beatrice!" he cried, and throwing himself on the earth beside her, he kissed her hand passionately. Her faintness began now to dissipate; but her reason did not return. The first words she uttered were those of madness; she raved of that which ever haunted her thoughts in delirium, her prison in Romagna. Tripalda heard the words, and started, as if he had trodden on a viper; his sallow complexion became paler,—but Castruccio did not attend to this, or make out her speech. He perceived her frenzy; and, unable any longer to endure his remorse, or the sight of his hapless victim, he gave hasty orders that she should be conveyed slowly and carefully to the palace of the countess of Valperga, and her companions be detained as prisoners; and then he rode off. He rode towards Lucca; and, reflecting on the fright that Euthanasia might sustain if she saw her unhappy friend brought home in so miserable a state, he resolved to go first to her palace, and inform her of what had passed.

"And are you come to this, lovely Beatrice?" he thought. "And is this the same creature, who, radiant with beauty and joy, formerly gave me her benediction at the palace of the good old Marsilio? I remember that day, as if it were yesterday; and now I find her with grey hairs and a wasted form, a young fruit utterly blighted, and, worse than all, her reason fallen the victim of her misery. Am I the cause of this?"

He rode on swiftly, and soon arrived at the palace. He did not reflect that he was going to behold Euthanasia, the beautiful and beloved; and thinking of nothing but Beatrice, and finding the gates open, he entered. It was about three in the morning. During the night Euthanasia had thought that she heard a groan come from the chamber of Beatrice; and she hastened thither, to discover if any new sorrow disturbed her unfortunate guest. The chamber was empty; the bed unslept upon; she sought her in the adjoining rooms; and, not finding her, she became terrified, and, rousing the house, had the palace searched, but in vain; no trace of her was left. She sent several messengers to different gates of the town to learn whether she had been seen, and waited with inexpressible anxiety for their return.

The prince found men consulting together in the great hall; and the first words he heard was the name of "Madonna Beatrice."

"Do not be alarmed," he said, coming forward. "I know where she is, and she will soon be here; some of you see that her couch be prepared, and seek a physician, for she is very ill. Where is the countess?"

Appearing thus unexpectedly and alone, the men did not recognize the prince; but the quick ear of Euthanasia caught the sound of his voice; and, coming out of an adjoining room, she cried, "Do you then know where my friend is, Castruccio?"

"I do indeed," he replied: "and it is fortunate; since I may have saved her from evil hands. But I am perfectly ignorant how and why she came to a spot so far from the town."

He related in a few words where and in what manner he had found her, and concluded by saying, "I leave her to your care; I know how kind and generous you are. If she recover, I intreat you to inform me without delay of so favourable a change."

As he said this, the trampling of horsemen was heard in the streets;—he cried, "I dare not see her again; farewell, Euthanasia; pity her and me!"

He hastened from the palace, and in a few minutes after Beatrice was brought in; her countenance was deadly pale, and her arms hung lifelessly over the shoulder of one of the men who supported her; her hair was dank, and her garments wetted with the dew of morning; her eyes were open, and glared meaninglessly around. They laid her on a bed; and Euthanasia, approaching, took her hand; Beatrice did not notice her; she seemed to have lost all sensation, and the rolling of her eyes, and the convulsive gaspings of her breath, were all the signs of life that she gave.

Why should I describe the scenes that ensued during the following days? Descriptions of unmixed horror cannot be pleasing; and what other feelings could mingle to soften that sensation, on beholding the declining state of poor Beatrice? She never again had any return of reason, nor did she ever sleep; generally she lay, as I have described, pale and motionless; if ever she woke to sensation, it was to rave and scream, so that the hardest heart might have been penetrated with excess of pity. Some have seen, most have read the descriptions of, madness. She called upon Euthanasia, upon Castruccio; but, more than all, she fancied that she was chained to her dungeon-floor in her tremendous prison, mocked and laughed at by her keepers; and sometimes she imagined that these beloved friends were chained beside her, suffering those torments which she had herself endured. She never in her wildest sallies uttered a reproachful word against Castruccio, although it appeared that she sometimes thought that he accused himself; and then with the tenderest accents, and most winning sweetness, she bade him not grieve, and assured him that he had committed no fault.

These intervals of raving were short and rare; and, as she became weaker, she still seldomer emerged from her state of insensibility. She was evidently dying; the physicians gave no hopes of her life; and the priests crowded about her. Padre Lanfranco was among them; and he bitterly reproached himself for having left her, and endeavoured to compensate for his neglect, by watching day and night for some return of reason, when he might ask whether she died in the faith of the church. This never arrived: but the priests were lenient; they placed the crucifix on her breast, and she seemed to press it; once, when the name of her Redeemer was mentioned, her eyes lighted up, and a smile seemed to play upon her lips. She was so perfectly senseless, that this could have had no connexion with the words that had been used; but the charitable priests chose to construe it into an enternal assurance of the salvation of her soul; and they administered the sacraments. She never spoke afterwards; but day by day she grew weaker; Castruccio sent continually to inquire of her state; but he dared not come. Euthanasia hardly ever left her bed side; and she became as pale, and almost as weak, as the dying Beatrice.

Such had been the effect of the witch's incantations. Beatrice had needed the tenderest nursing; and she had received instead, a shock which saner nerves than hers could hardly have sustained. Yet her death was smoothed to her by the affectionate ministry of her friend; and she at last lost all sense even of pain. She died, peacefully, and calmly as a child; and her many sorrows and wrongs no longer filled her with anguish and despair. She died: Euthanasia was beside her when she heard a gentle sigh, followed by a fixedness of feature and rigidity of limb, which shewed that the mighty change had taken place in her frame.

Tears and lamentation succeeded to her death. Euthanasia wished that her funeral should be private and unnoticed; but Castruccio insisted that it should be attended with every circumstance of pomp used in those days. The room was hung with black cloth, and made as dark as night, to give brightness to the many torches by which it was illuminated. Beatrice was laid on a bier, arrayed in costly apparel, and canopied with a pall of black velvet embroidered with gold: flowers, whose beauty and freshness mocked the livid hues of the corpse, were strewn over her, and scattered about the room; and two boys walked about, swinging censers of incense. The chamber was filled with mourning women; one, the chief, dressed in black, with dishevelled hair, knelt near the head of the bier, and began the funeral song; she sang a strain in monotonous, but not unmelodious voice: the verses were extempore, and described the virtues and fortunes of the deceased; they ended with the words:

Oime! ora giace morta sulla bara! [3]

And the other women, taking up the burthen, cried in shrill tones:

Oime! ora giace morta sulla bara!

Again they were silent: and the *Cantatrice*, renewing her song, repeated another verse in praise of poor Beatrice. Castruccio had told her in part what ought to be the subject of her song. The first verse described her as beautiful, beloved and prosperous, among her friends and fellow citizens: "Then," cried the singer, "the spoiler came; she lost all that was dear to her; and she wandered forth a wretch upon the earth. Who can tell what she suffered? Evil persons were abroad; they seized on her; and she became the victim of unspoken crimes: worse ills followed, madness and heresy, which threatened to destroy her soul."

The woman wept, wept unfeigned tears as she sang; and the hired mourners sympathized in her grief; each verse ended with the words,

Oime! ora giace morta sulla bara!

which were echoed by them all, and accompanied by cries and tears.

She ended; and, night being come, the hour for interment arrived. The censers were replenished with incense; and the priests sprinkled holy water about the room. Four lay-brothers raised the bier, and followed a troop of priests and monks, who went first with the crucifix, chaunting a *De profundis*. The streets through which they passed, were rendered as light as day by the glare of torches; after the priests, came the bier on which the body lay exposed, covered with flowers; many of the young girls and women of the city followed, each carrying a wax taper; a troop of horse closed the procession. It was midnight when they entered the church; the moon threw the shadow of the high window on the pavement; but all shadows were effaced by the torches which filled the church. Beatrice was laid in her peaceful grave; and, mass being said for the repose of her soul, the ceremony closed.

Euthanasia had not been present: and, although she longed for solitude to weep in peace over the fate of her hapless friend, she was obliged to receive the visits of the Lucchese ladies, who came to condole with her on this occasion, and perhaps to satisfy their curiosity concerning its object. The funeral feast was sumptuous and well attended, though few knew in whose honour it was given. Euthanasia shrunk from their questions, and was angry with Castruccio, that he should have placed her in so disagreeable a situation. It seemed to her better to befit the hapless fate of Beatrice, that she should have been permitted to depart unmarked, wept only by those, who knew her worth, and who lamented her unequaled misfortunes. It was the false pride of Castruccio, that made him think differently; and such were the prejudices of the times, that his contemporaries would have agreed with him, that he had in some degree compensated for the injuries that Beatrice had received from him, by the magnificence of her funeral.

After the ceremony was ended, Castruccio first thought of the two individuals whom he had found in the forest with their victim. Mandragola had preserved an uniform silence; and no threats, nor torture itself, could induce her to speak. Bindo was formed of frailer clay; she had charged him not to reveal what had passed, and had imprecated the most terrible curses on his head, if he disobeyed. He trembled; but the sight of the instruments of torture overcame him, and he confessed all. Mandragola was condemned by the laws which then existed in every country against the dealers in the black art, and suffered death as a witch. Euthanasia endeavoured to procure the freedom of the Albinois; but in vain. He was confined in the dungeons of the Dominican convent; he pined for liberty; and in a few months he died.

The tie which bound Euthanasia to Lucca, was now broken. For many days she sorrowed, forgetful of herself, over the fate of her friend. By degrees however the feelings of actual life returned to her; and she longed to quit a town, which had been for her the theatre of tremendous misfortune. Two months after the death of Beatrice she returned to Florence; where she found, in the society of her friends, and in the cultivation of her mind, some alleviation for her sorrow, and some compensation for the many evils she had endured.

[2] Jusquiamo [henbane: hebenon, *Shakespear*] was the principal ingredient in these intoxicating draughts. They had the property of producing madness.

[3] Alas! she now lies dead upon the bier!

CHAPTER VIII

Castruccio had now been lord of Lucca for six years, and had attained his thirty-third year; his character was formed; and his physiognomy, changed from its youthful expression, had become impressed by his habitual feelings. Constant exposure to the sun and weather had tinged his cheek with brown; which, but for that, had been deadly pale; for care, and the strong emotions to which he was subject, had left their mark on his countenance; his eye had grown hollow, and the smooth lustre of his brow was diminished by lines, which indeed looked gracefully at his years, since they marked the progress of thought; but some, more straggling and undefined, shewed that those passions whose outward signs he suppressed, yet preyed upon the vital principle; his eyes had not lost their fire, but their softness was gone.

He was kind and even grateful to his friends, so long as he considered them as such; but he was quick to distrust; and cold looks and averted favour followed suspicion: if these were answered by aught but patience and submission, hatred quickly came, and that never failed to destroy its object. If he only suspected, that was sufficient cause, that he who had become thus obnoxious to his prince should be told that it was his will that he should instantly depart from Lucca; and the confiscation filled the public coffers. If he thought that he had reason to fear, the doom of that man whom he feared was sealed: he was cruel and unrelenting; and the death of his victim did not satisfy him; several were starved to death by his command, and worse tortures were inflicted upon others:—something of this was to be attributed to the usage of the times; but cruelty had become an elemental feature of Castruccio's character.

If he were feared by his enemies in open war, his secret policy was still more dreaded. He had not forgotten the lessons of Alberto Scoto; and, as his attempt on the life of the king of Naples might prove, his measures had perhaps been influenced by the counsels of Benedetto Pepi. He had many spies in each town, and collected intelligence from every court of Lombardy. Women and priests were his frequent instruments; and even the more distinguished among the citizens were induced through his largesses to betray the counsels of their country.

Such was Antelminelli, the some time lover of Euthanasia; daring, artful, bounteous and cruel; evil predominated in his character; and, if he were loved by a few, he was hated by most, and feared by all. His perpetual wars, which impoverished the neighbouring states, did not enrich his own; his artful policy sowed distrust among dear friends, and spies and traitors abounded during his reign. In Lucca he was as an eagle in a cage; he had a craving that seemed to demand the empire of the world; and, weak as he was in means and hopes, he made the nations tremble.

The object of Castruccio's present policy was Florence. He proceeded by measured steps; but he was perpetually gaining some advantage against the rival state, improving his military discipline, and preparing for the last assault. His first attempt was upon Pistoia, and he carried this place by a double treachery. The Florentines took the alarm upon so disastrous an event; and the pope sent to them Raymond de Cardona, one of the most eminent generals of the times, whom they immediately placed at the head of their armies. Cardona crossed the Guisciana, and ravaged the plain of Lucca, which had for many years been unspoiled by the hostile sword; but, when it became necessary for him to retreat, Castruccio by masterly movements intercepted his march, obtained a complete victory, and, after a short, but severe contest, took Cardona and all his army prisoners.

The battle of this day was called the field of Altopascio. Arrigo Guinigi was among the slain; and his loss was grievously felt by Castruccio. The prince of Lucca had ever looked on him as a treasure consigned to him by his late father; and, amidst all his faults, Castruccio preserved his gratitude for the lessons of that admirable man, and a sweet remembrance of the days of peace he had passed with him among the Euganean hills. He had loved Arrigo, as a dear brother, or a son; childless himself, he sometimes thought, that, although there was small difference between their ages, Arrigo would succeed him, that his children would be his heirs, and that, if not bound to him by the ties of blood, yet they would look back to him with the same gratitude and respect, that an honoured posterity regard the founder of their house. Ambition hardens the heart; but such is the texture of the mind of man, that he is constantly urged to contemplate those days, when his once over-awing sceptre shall have fallen from his nerveless grasp; the worst usurper, as he advances in years, looks with tenderness on his children, who, in the peaceful exercise of power, are to efface the memory of the lawless deeds by which he had acquired it. Castruccio saw the son of Guinigi in this light, and he felt a pang of sincere and deep grief, when it became his turn to heap his grassy tomb, amidst the many others with which the plain around Altopascio was crowded, and to order the place where the remains of Arrigo reposed, to be marked with a sepulchral pillar.

From Altopascio, Castruccio advanced with his army to the very gates of Florence. The peasants fled before him, and took refuge, with what property they could save, in the city; the rest became the prey of the Lucchese army, who marked their progress by fire and devastation. All the harvests had been brought in; but Castruccio's soldiers wreaked their vengeance upon the fields, tearing up and burning the vines, cutting down the olive woods, seizing or burning the winter-stock, and reducing the cottages of the poor to a heap of formless ruins. The country about Florence was adorned by numerous villas, the summer abodes of the rich citizens, ornamented with all the luxury of the times, the grounds laid out in the most delicious gardens, where beautiful trees and flowers adorned the landscape, and natural and artificial rills and waterfalls diffused coolness in the midst of summer. These became the prey of the soldier; the palaces were ransacked, and afterwards burned; the cultivated grounds covered with ruins, the rivulets choked up, and all that, a few days before, had presented the show of a terrestrial paradise, now appeared as if an earthquake, mocking the best cares of man, had laid it in ruin.

The army encamped before the gates of Florence. The remnant of the troops of Cardona and the remainder of the citizens capable of bearing arms, would have formed a force sufficient to cope with the army of Antelminelli. But more than their declared enemies, the Florentines feared domestic traitors; so many of their first citizens were prisoners to the prince of Lucca, that they dreaded lest their relations might endeavour to secure for them their freedom even by the betraying of their native city. Day and night they guarded the walls and gates, and patroled the streets, each regarding the other with suspicious eyes, and listening with fear and horror to the sounds of rejoicing and riot that issued from the camp of Castruccio.

The prince, in contempt and derision of the besieged, encouraged every kind of pastime and insulting mockery, that might sting his proud, though humbled enemies: he instituted games and races, coined money, and sent continual defiances to the citizens to issue from their walls and encounter him in battle. The men, too ready to seize the spirit of hatred and ridicule, amused themselves with casting by means of their *balestri*, the carcases of dead asses and dogs into the town. Woe to the Florentine who fell into their hands; if a female, no innocence nor tears could save her from their brutality, and, if a man, if their insults were less cruel, they were hardly less cutting and humiliating; to lead a prisoner naked through the camp, seated on an ass, with his face turned towards the tail, was a common mockery. Castruccio perhaps did not perceive the full extent to which the brutal ferocity of his soldiers, made drunk by victory, carried them; if he did, he winked at it; for he had not that magnanimity which should lead him to treat with respect and kindness a fallen enemy.

While the Lucchese soldiers rioted in plenty, filling themselves even to satiety with the delicate wines and food of the Florentine nobles, and consuming in a few weeks the provision of years, the inhabitants of the besieged city presented a far different spectacle. The villagers, driven from their cottages, had taken refuge in Florence, whose gates jealously closed, permitted not the means of subsistence to be increased. In consequence of this, of the supernumerary population of the town, and of the unwholesome food on which the poorer classes were forced to subsist, pestilence and other contagious fevers declared themselves: the streets were filled with mournful processions, the bells tolled a perpetual knell of death; the citizens invited their friends to the funeral feasts, but the seats of many of the guests were vacated by death, and the hosts who celebrated them had been invited to several similar commemorations. Every face looked blank and fearful. The magistrates were obliged to interfere; they issued an order that the relations of the dead were no longer to celebrate their funerals by assemblies of their friends, or to toll the bell during the ceremony, so that the numerous dead might go to their long homes without terrifying the survivors by their numbers. Yet this law could not hide the works of death that were so frequent in the town; the streets were almost deserted, except by the monks, who hurried from house to house carrying the cross and sacrament to the dying; while the poor, almost starving, and often houseless, fell in the streets, or were carried in terrifying troops to the hospitals and convents of charity. And this was the work of Castruccio.

Euthanasia saw and felt this; and she felt as if, bound to him by an indissoluble chain, it was her business to follow, like an angel, in his track, to heal the wounds that he inflicted. Dressed in a coarse garb, and endeavouring to throw aside those feelings of delicacy which were as a part of her, she visited the houses of the poor, aided the sick, fed the hungry, and would perform offices that even wives and mothers shrunk from with disgust and fear. An heroic sentiment possessed her mind, and lifted her above humanity; she must atone for the crimes of him she had loved.

Bondelmonti one day visited her; she had just returned from closing the eyes of an unhappy woman, whose husband and children had fled from their mother and wife, in the fear of infection; she had changed her garments on entering the palace, and lay on a couch, exhausted; for she had not slept for the two previous nights. Bondelmonti approached her unperceived, and kissed her hand;—she drew it away: "Beware!" she said. "If you knew from whence I came, you would not touch a hand that may carry infection with it."

Bondelmonti reproached her for the carelessness with which she exposed her health and her life: but Euthanasia interrupted him: "I thank you, dear cousin, for your anxiety; but you know me of old, and will not attempt to deter me from doing that which I regard as my duty.— —But what would you now say to me; for I perceive weighty thought in your overhanging brow?"

"Am I not like the rest of our townsmen in that? You see, Madonna, perhaps better than any of us, to what straits our city is reduced, while this Lucchese tyrant triumphs; you perceive our miseries too well not to pity them; and I trust that you are too good a patriot not to desire most earnestly to put an end to them."

"My dear friend, what do you say? I would sacrifice my life, and more than life, to be of use to my fellow citizens. God knows how deeply I lament their defeats and their unhappiness. But what can be done? An angel alone could inspire our troops with that spirit and courage, which would fit them to cope with the forces of the prince."

"You say true; but there are other means for overthrowing him. Consider, Euthanasia, that not only he conquers and despoils us, but that he is a cruel and bloody tyrant, execrated by the chiefs of our religion, feared and hated by all who approach him, one whose death would spread joy and exultation over all Italy."

"His death!" Euthanasia's pale cheek became still paler.

"Nay, you are a woman; and, in spite of your superior strength of mind, I see that you are still to be frightened by words. Do not let us therefore talk of his death, but only of his overthrow; we must contrive that."

Euthanasia remained silent. Bondelmonti continued:

"Call to mind, Madonna, the many excellent and virtuous persons whom he has murdered. I need not mention your friend Leodino, or any other individual; his enemies have fallen beneath his axe like trees in a forest; and he feels as little remorse as the woodman who fells them. Torture, confiscation, treachery and ingratitude have gone hand in hand with murder. Before he came, Lucca belonged to the Guelphs, and peace hovered over Tuscany. Now the first nobles of the land have either fallen victims to his jealousy, or wander as beggars in Italy. All that is virtuous and worthy under his dominion send up daily prayers for his downfall; and that is now near at hand; the means are ready, the instruments are preparing— —"

"For his death?" cried Euthanasia.

"Nay, if you intercede for him, he may be saved: but it must be upon one condition."

"What is that?"

"That you join our conspiracy, and aid its accomplishment; thus Antelminelli may be saved, otherwise his fate is sealed. Consider this alternative; you may take a week for reflection on what I have said."

Bondelmonti left her. The sleep that had been about to visit her wearied senses, fled far away,—scared by the doubts and anguish that possessed her heart.

She felt with double severity this change from the calm that she had enjoyed for the three preceding years, into the fears and miseries of a struggle to which she saw no end. The tyranny and warlike propensities of Castruccio were so entirely in opposition to every feeling of her heart, that she would not have lamented his fall; especially as then perhaps she would have conceived it her duty to stand near him in misfortune, to console his disappointed hopes, and to teach him the lesson of content in obscurity. But to join the conspiracy, to become one of those who plotted against him, to assist in directing the blow which should annihilate, if not his life, at least all that he regarded as necessary to his happiness, was a task she shuddered at being called upon to fulfil.

No one can act conscientiously up to his sense of duty, or perhaps go even beyond that sense, in the exercise of benevolence and self-sacrifice, without being repaid by the sweetest and most secure happiness that man can enjoy, self-approbation. Euthanasia had devoted herself for some weeks to the nursing the sick, and the feeding of the hungry; and her benevolence was repaid by a return of healthful spirits and peace of mind, which it seemed that no passing circumstance of life could disturb. It was in vain that she witnessed scenes of pain and wretchedness; she felt that pity which angels are said to feel; but so strange is the nature of the human mind, that the most unblemished serenity reigned in her soul. Her sleep, when she found time to sleep, was deep and refreshing; as she moved, she felt as if she were air, there was so much elasticity and lightness of spirit in her motions and her thoughts. She shed tears, as she heard the groans and complaints of the sufferers; but she felt as if she were lifted beyond their sphere, and that her soul, clothed in garments of heavenly texture, could not be tarnished with earthly dross. All this was now changed. She fell again into weak humanity, doubting, fearing, hoping.

When Castruccio's army removed from before the walls of Florence, the gates were thrown open, and its inhabitants were relieved from the pressure and burthen of supernumerary inhabitants. But where did the peasant go?

he found his cottage burnt, his vines, his next year's hope, destroyed, ghastly ruin stared him in the face, and his countenance reflected back the horrors of a long train of misery that he saw was preparing for him. Euthanasia could do little good amidst the universal devastation; what she could do, she did. She restricted her own expenditure, and all the money she could collect, was expended on the relief of these poor people; but this was a small pittance, a drop of water in the ocean of their calamities.

She was returning from one of these visits to the country, where she had been struck with horror to perceive the inadequacy of her aid to the miseries around her. A whole village had been laid waste, the implements of husbandry destroyed, the cattle carried off, and there was neither food for the starving inhabitants, nor hope of an harvest for the ensuing year. She had heard the name of Antelminelli loaded with such imprecations as a father's mind suggested, when his children called on him vainly for food, and Castruccio the cause of this misery. "If God fulfils," she thought, "as they say he does, the curses of the injured, how will *his* soul escape, weighed down by the imprecations of thousands? Yet I will not consent to the hopes of his enemies, nor be instrumental in dragging him from his seat of power. I have loved him; and what would be just vengeance in another, would be treachery and black ingratitude in me. Ingratitude! And yet for what? For lost hopes, content destroyed, and confidence in virtue shaken. These are the benefits I have received from him; yet I will not join his enemies."

On her return to her palace, she found Bondelmonti waiting for her. "Have you decided?" he asked.

"I have. I cannot enter into your conspiracy."

"Do you know, Madonna, that in deciding thus you sign his death-warrant?"

"Nay, cousin, it is ungenerous and unmanly to use such a menace with me. If he be doomed to death, which indeed cannot, must not be, — — how can I save him? how can I, a woman, turn aside the daggers of the conspirators? if it be not indeed by betraying your plot to him, a deed you may perhaps force me to at last."

"I hope not, Euthanasia. For your own sake—for the sake of all the virtue that ever dwelt beneath the female form, I hope that you will not be led to commit so base an action. You cannot harm us. If you inform Antelminelli that there is a conspiracy formed against him, and that I am at the head of it, you tell him no more than he already knows. He does not need the lessons of history; his own experience teaches him sufficiently, that the sword is suspended over the tyrant's head by a single hair. He knows that he has enemies; but he has too many to arrest them all: he knows that his friends are treacherous; but he will never guess who on the present occasion will turn traitor. He cannot be surprised, nor can it do him any good to know, that I am the chief conspirator; I have ever been his open and determined foe; and this is not my first attempt to accomplish his downfal.

"As to what you say concerning my childish menace, you much misunderstand me when you call it a threat. The persons who must act in this business are Lucchese; I may direct their exertions; but they are the actors. And, if you heard the appalling curses that they heap upon Castruccio's name, if you beheld the deep hate their eyes express when he is mentioned, their savage joy when they dream that one day they may wreak their vengeance upon him, you would feel that his life is indeed at stake. I do not wish him to die. Perhaps I am wrong in this; if his life be preserved, it is probable that no good will arise from his downfall and that no blood will in reality be spared. But I have eaten at his board, and he has been my guest within these walls, so that I would preserve his life; and I have pitched upon you as the person who can best assist me in this. What else can I do? I cannot go to Lucca to watch over and restrain the fury of his enemies; nor can I find one Lucchese to whom I dare disclose the secret of the conspiracy, and whom I may trust with the protection of his person. Indeed this task seems naturally to devolve to you. You hate tyranny and war; you are a Guelph, and would fain see the enemy of your country, the author of the innumerable evils under which we groan, removed from his government: but antient friendship, the reciprocal interchange of hospitality render his person dear to you, and your female softness, and perhaps weakness, would come in aid of these feelings. You are free to go to Lucca; you may mix the voice of humanity with the bloody machinations of these men; you may save him, and you alone."

Euthanasia was deeply moved by the representations of Bondelmonti. But her thoughts were still confused; she saw no steady principle, on which to seize, and make it her guide from out the labyrinth. She paused, hesitated, and asked again for a few days for consideration. And this Bondelmonti reluctantly granted.

In the mean time Castruccio was engaged in exhibiting the pomp of a triumph, which was conducted with unparalleled splendour; and in which, like a merciless barbarian, the prince of Lucca, led along Cardona and all the most eminent of his prisoners as the attendants of his chariot.

CHAPTER IX

During this festivity at Lucca, every thing wore the face of sorrow and depression at Florence. The only circumstance that raised them from their ruin, was the commerce of the city; for, by means of the merchants, corn was brought from the neighbouring states, and the magistrates distributed it among the poorer peasantry.

Euthanasia had listened to the intelligence of Castruccio's triumph with unwilling ears. It seemed to her like the pomp of his funeral; and she dreaded lest his person, exposed during the ceremonial, should be attempted by some of his bolder enemies. But they worked with a closer design.

The tide of her sensations turned, when the conclusion of that day's pomp brought nothing with it, but the account of its splendour and success; and, when she heard that the prince was personally safe, she found fresh reason for regret, in the want of that delicate and honourable feeling on his part, which above all her other virtues characterised her own mind.

But, if she were disgusted by the low pride that Castruccio manifested in his treatment of Cardona, her feelings of horror and of hatred were called forth by the occurrences that followed. Four days after this scene Bondelmonti entered her apartment: his manner was abrupt; his face pale; he could not speak.—When he had somewhat recovered, his first words were a torrent of execrations against Antelminelli.

"Oh, cease!" cried Euthanasia, "you hate, and would destroy, but do not curse him!"

"Bid me rather add tenfold bitterness to my weak execrations; but all words man can pronounce are poor. He has done that which, if he had before been an angel, would blot and disfigure him for ever. He is the worst of tyrants, the most cruel and atrocious wretch that breathes! But earth shall soon be rid of the monster. Read that writing!"

He put into her hand a dirty scrap of paper, on which she deciphered these words:

"For holy Jesu's sake, save me! My mother does not send my ransom. I was put to the torture this morning. I suffer it again on Thursday, if you do not send six hundred golden florins.

"Pity your FRANCESCO BONDELMONTI."

The paper dropt from her hands. "This comes from my cousin Francesco," said Bondelmonti; "others are in the same situation. Those who have not been ransomed, he has thrown into the most loathsome dungeons, and starves and tortures them to quicken their appetite for freedom. Shall such a one reign?"

"No," cried Euthanasia, her cheek burning with indignation, and her lips quivering with excessive pity; "No, he shall not reign; he were unworthy to live, if it be not to repent. Bondelmonti, here is my hand; do with me what you please; let his life be saved; but let him be torn from the power which he uses more like a fiend than a human creature."

"Thank you, dear cousin, for this generous feeling: now I know you again. I know my Euthanasia, who had forgotten herself awhile, only to awake again with new vigour. Call up all your spirits, Madonna; recollect all of noble, and wise, and courageous, that your excellent father taught you. This is no may-day trick, or the resolution of momentary indignation; it is the firm purpose of those, who see an evil beyond imagination pregnant with destruction and horror. Your quick concession merits my utmost confidence; and you shall have it. To-night I will see you again. Now I must endeavour to borrow money to liberate Francesco. My purse has been emptied by the ransom of my three brothers, and his mother has three hundred florins only."

"I can supply the rest," said Euthanasia. "Poor fellow, send them immediately; that with the shortest delay he may be rescued from the power of one more remorseless than the rack on which he suffers. To-night I see you again."

Euthanasia spent the intervening hours in great agitation. She did not shrink from her purpose; she had given her word, and she did not dream of recalling it. But all was turmoil and confusion in her mind. She figured to herself the scenes that would ensue; she imagined the downfal of him she had loved, his life saved only through her intervention,—and he perhaps, knowing that she also had joined the conspiracy to despoil him of the power he had laboured to attain, would turn from her in abhorrence.

As she thought of this, a few natural tears fell; she cast her deep blue eyes up to heaven; and tried to collect all her fortitude. Night came, and with it the hour when she expected Bondelmonti; but all was tumult and uneasiness in her heart: and to all other regrets she added the startling doubt whether she were not on the present occasion quitting the path of innocence, for the intricate and painful one of error. Then she knelt down, and prayed fervently for a wisdom and judgement that might guide her aright.

Euthanasia was now advanced to the very prime of life. Ten years had elapsed since she had first interchanged vows with Antelminelli in her castle of Valperga; but her mind was of that youthful kind, that, ever, as it were, renewing itself from her own exhaustless treasure of wisdom and sentiment, never slept upon the past, forgetful of the changes that took place around her. Her character was always improving, always adding some new acquirements, or strengthening those which she possessed before; and thus for ever enlarging her sphere of knowledge and feeling. She often felt as if she were not the same being that she had been a few years before; she often figured to herself, that it was only from such or such a period that she obtained a true insight into the affairs of life, and became initiated in real wisdom; but these epochs were continually changing, for day by day she experienced the acquisition of some new power, the discovery of some new light which guided her through the labyrinth, while another of the thousand-folded veils which hide the sun of reality from the ardent spirit of youth, fell before her piercing gaze. Yet the change that she felt in her faculties was greater than that which had really taken place; it was only the disclosure of another petal of the blowing rose, but the bud had contained the germ of all that appeared as if new-created.

With this matured judgement and depth of feeling, she was called upon to take an arduous part in a most doubtful and perilous undertaking. The enthusiasm that distinguished her, had ever induced her to place a great confidence in her own sentiments, and the instantaneous decision of any doubtful point; and now she did not hesitate in resolving to become one in the conspiracy: her refusal would not stop its progress; her consent would enable her to judge of, and regulate its measures. She no longer loved the prince; his cruelty had degraded him even from the small place that he had still kept in her heart. But such was the force of early feeling, that she desired to restore her affections to him, when he should again become gentle and humane, as he appeared when she first knew him. Adversity might bring about this change.

Bondelmonti appeared. He appeared with a face of satisfaction and even of joy, as he claimed her promise of the morning. She renewed it solemnly, while her serious countenance, and the touching modulation of her voice, told how from the depth of her heart she felt the extent and force of the engagement into which she entered. Bondelmonti then detailed to her the circumstances of the conspiracy.

The family of the Quartezzani had been that which had most assisted Castruccio in his rise to power, and had stood by him long with fidelity. But, as his tyranny became more secure, he feared their power, more than he was pleased by their support, and supected that they only looked upon him as an instrument to fight their battles awhile, and then to be put aside at the first opportunity. He changed his demeanour towards them, from that of friendliness, to the coldest distrust, and took the earliest opportunity to banish the chief among them from Lucca. Disgusted by this ingratitude, they withdrew from court, and tempted by the emissaries of Bondelmonti, now entered into a conspiracy against him, joining with the Avogadii, his professed enemies, to despoil him of power, perhaps of life.

Bondelmonti explained to Euthanasia all the circumstances of the plan they had concerted to get the city into their hands. The present governor of Pisa, who remembered, and hated the prince on account of the treason he had fomented against him, was to advance in a hostile manner to Ripafrata; and, while the shew of force on that side should attract Castruccio and his army, a detachment was to cross the hill of St. Giuliano, and come suddenly on the city, whose gates would be opened to them by one of the conspirators. The Florentine force would hover on the banks of the Guisciana; and, taking advantage of the confusion which the seizure of Lucca would occasion, would pass the river, and march directly towards the city, declaring liberty to the peasant, and attacking the partizans of the tyrant alone. King Robert of Naples had a fleet already in the gulph of Spezia, which, on the news of the breaking out of the conspiracy, would disembark its soldiers on the Lucchese territory, and thus add to the general confusion.

This was the outline of the plan; there were many smaller circumstances which Bondelmonti detailed. He then named their associates in the plot. In calling over the list he mentioned Tripalda; Euthanasia's eyes flashed angrily at the sound of that name.

"Tripalda!" she cried, "Battista Tripalda! Is he one of your associates? Nay then, I am truly sorry that I am now numbered among you."

"Why this passion, my fair cousin? Tripalda is a man of infinite talent: his counsels have been of the greatest benefit to us. I do not think that our plot would ever have ripened into maturity, had it not been for him. Of what consequence is the virtue or vice of a man on such an occasion? Edged tools are what we want; it matters little the evil name with which they may be branded."

"You reason ill, my friend; and, if you persist, I foresee the failure of our plan, and the destruction of those engaged in it. I have promised my assistance, nor will I shrink from the task imposed upon me; but I can no longer have faith in our success, if one so treacherous and unprincipled as Tripalda be admitted into a participation of our counsels. Accident has made me acquainted with the full extent of his crimes; it is the knowledge of them that has caused his expulsion from the palace and society of the prince, his crimes alone impel him to associate in this conspiracy, and they also ought to induce us to reject him; that cause must be bad, which requires the assistance of one so wicked as this infidel priest."

"You are strangely prejudiced, methinks, against this man," replied Bondelmonti, "but indeed, my dear cousin, such as he is, we must now tolerate him. He is not only acquainted with every circumstance of the conspiracy, but has been its most active member. Many of our most valuable partizans have been gained over by him alone; he is the tie which binds those who are personally at variance one with the other, and the stay which fixes the fluctuating."

"And this then is the trap into which we are about to fall? This man hates the prince, because Castruccio is fully acquainted with the extent of his iniquity; for the same reason he detests me— —"

"This expression of yours," interrupted Bondelmonti, "proves the excess of your misapprehension. So far from disliking, he esteems and admires you, and it was at his instigation that I first named our purpose to you."

"All that you say, unfortunately increases my distrust. But, if, as I believe, I have done well in promising my assistance, fear shall not withhold me from exerting my powers, and giving my whole heart to the undertaking. My dear Bondelmonti, you are the oldest of my friends, you were the friend of my father, I trust much to your judgement; I confide greatly in the sense of right which nature has implanted in my own heart; I hope no false view, no veiled passion, misleads me now, when most I desire to act well, justly towards others, and towards myself: the catastrophe is in the hands of that irresistible Power which guides us all; and, if we fail, no weakness, no vain reproach, or worse treachery, shall tarnish my defeat. Trust in me to the death."

CHAPTER X

One of the first effects of Euthanasia's entrance into the conspiracy of Bondelmonti, was a journey from Florence to Lucca. It was necessary for her to be there some time before the breaking out of the plot, that she might be able to take the part allotted to her. She quitted her native city with a heavy heart. It was at the end of the month of November; and the lowering skies portended rain, and the bare earth, stripped of its summer ornaments, appeared chilled by the cold blast that passed over it. The olive and ilex woods, and the few cork trees and cypresses, that grew on the declivities of the hills, diversified the landscape with their sober green: but they had a funereal appearance; they were as the pall of the dying year, and the melancholy song of their waving branches was its dirge.

Euthanasia's mind was no store-house of blithe thoughts. She felt deeply the danger of the project in which she had embarked; and yet its danger was one of the considerations that reconciled her to it. To have encountered Castruccio with superior force, and to have despoiled him of all power with security to herself, would have been hateful to her feelings; and it appeared to her that in acting such a part she would have merited the disapprobation of mankind. But she approached the foundations of his power by a path encompassed with danger; she groped through the murky air of night, and owls and bats flitted before her, and flapped their wings in her eyes; her footing was unsteady;—a precipice yawned on each side, and the probable result of her undertaking was ignominy and death. She felt all this. The name of Tripalda had extinguished in her bosom every hope of success. She felt that the purity of her intentions would excuse her in her own eyes; and she could then endure with patience all of bitter and evil that might befal her. She could not say in the words of the poet,

> Roll on, the chariot-wheels of my dear plots,
> And bear mine ends to their desired marks!
> As yet there's not a rub of wit, or gulph of thought,
> No rocky misconstruction, thorny maze,
> Or other let of any doubtfulness:
> As yet thy way is smooth and plain,
> Like the green ocean in a silent calm [4] .

No! the course she followed was a slippery path, that overhung a chasm terrible as death: the sea on which she sailed was rife with quicksands, and its breakers threatened instant destruction.

Sometimes the memory of her peaceful life at Florence obtruded itself upon her, and more than that, her charitable occupations when she attended the sick in that city, and whence, as from a rough-hewn chalice containing nectarian drink, she had quaffed happiness. Sometimes she reproached destiny that she had not fallen a victim to her perilous exertions; but she endeavoured to shut out these remembrances from her mind, to look before her and not behind. What though dense clouds hid the future, and thunder muttered above? she was borne on by a virtuous purpose, which would be to her as the wings of an eagle, or the sure foot of the precipice-walking chamois.

And then, if the enterprise succeeded, she would save Castruccio. But for her he would be sacrificed by his insatiable enemies. But her hand would avert their daggers, her voice bid them "Hold!" — —Her imagination pictured the whole scene. He would be seized by his enemies, and expect death; he would be conveyed aboard one of the vessels of the king of Naples; and she would be there, to watch over and tend upon him. At first he might repulse, perhaps spurn her: but patient forbearance, and her meek demeanour would soften him; he would see the tears of her devotion; he would hear her defence; and he would forgive her. They would disembark on some lovely island on the sea of Baiæ—his prison. A resting-place, whose walls would be the ocean, and whose bars and locks the all-encompassing air—would be allotted to him on the island of Ischia. Thence he would survey the land where the philosophers of past ages lived; he would study their lessons; and their wisest lore would descend into his soul, like the dews of heaven upon the parched frame of the wanderer in the Arabian desarts. By degrees he would love obscurity. They would behold together the wondrous glories of the heavens, and the beauty of that transparent sea, whose floor of pebbles, shells and weeds, is as a diamond-paved palace of romance, shone on and illustrated as it is by the sun's rays. He would see the flame arise from Vesuvius, and behold afar off the smoke of the burning lava,—such was the emblem of his former life; but he would then have become, like the land he trod, an extinguished volcano; and the soil would prove more fertile, more rich in beauty and excellence, than those cold natures which had never felt the vivifying heat of mighty and subdued passions.

Thus she dreamed; and thus she cheated herself into tranquillity. She arrived at Pisa, where she was met by Orlando Quartezzani, who explained to her much of the minutiæ of the plot, and besought her to hasten its execution. "I pine, in exile," he said, "still to behold that ungrateful tyrant seated on a throne, which, if it be not formed of our skulls, yet exists only to torture and destroy us. My brothers are tardy, those Avogadii, lazy and inert. They are still at Lucca; they see its fertile vallies; they live among its mountains. Sometimes indeed I dare go to the top of the hill of San Giuliano, and behold its towers almost at my feet; but I long to make one with my fellow-citizens, to enter again into the lists of life."

Euthanasia quitted Pisa. She crossed the plain to the foot of the hills, and passed along through Pugnano and Ripafrata. She was very melancholy. How could it be otherwise? She had entered upon a race, whose penalty was death, whose prize was yet hidden in the mists of futurity;—it might turn out even more blighting and terrible than death itself. But there was no room for retreat; the path was narrow, and her chariot could not turn; she must fix her eyes upon the goal, for be the consequence good or evil, she must arrive there, she must there seek and find the fulfilment of her destiny.

She entered Lucca at the beginning of the month of December; and she went immediately to the palace which had been assigned her by the Lucchese government, in compensation for her demolished castle. The same evening that she arrived, the two chiefs of the conspiracy, Ugo Quartezzani and Tripalda, visited her. The name of Tripalda, so often and so fearfully repeated by the dying Beatrice, made her shrink from all communication with one who had tarnished his life with the foulest crimes. On this occasion she was obliged however to smother her indignation; and he, from a sense of his own importance, was more presumptuous and insolent than she had ever seen him.

"Madonna," said he, stalking forward with an erect mien, and half shut eyes, which, although they were not bent on the ground, yet ever avoided the direct gaze of those to whom he spoke;—"Madonna, I much praise your wisdom in entering into this conspiracy. We all know that, when you choose to exert your abilities, you are the cleverest woman in Tuscany. This is a period which will shew you in your true colours."

"Mester Battista, let us leave to speak of me and my poor talents: we come to talk of far weightier matter; and I bear a message to Messer Ugo from his brother Orlando."

They now began to speak of the future; but Tripalda would allow no one to talk but himself; and he walked up and down the room delivering his opinion in a loud voice.

"Hush, for Jesu's sake!" cried Ugo, "some one will overhear us, and we are all lost."

Tripalda looked suspiciously around, approached on tiptoe the sopha on which Euthanasia and Ugo sat, and, speaking in a whisper, he said,—"I tell you we shall succeed. Look! I have already sharpened the dagger which is to stab the tyrant to the heart."

"Now the Mother of God defend him!" cried Euthanasia, turning pale: "that is beyond my contract. Bear witness, Ugo, that I entered into this plot on condition that his life should be saved."

"Women! women!" said Tripalda, contemptuously. "By the body of Bacchus! I wonder what Bondelmonti meant by introducing a woman into the plot. One way or another they have spoiled, and ever will spoil, every design that the wisdom of man has contrived. I say he must die."

"I say he shall not, sir priest. And remember, you are not one who dares place your warrant on the life of Antelminelli. That is guarded by spirits of whose very existence you are ignorant; it is guarded by devoted love and disinterested virtue; and you shall not endanger it."

"You indeed talk of spirits, of which I and all the wise among men know nothing. In the present case I do not exactly see what devoted love has to do with a conspiracy to overthrow the party beloved; and as for disinterested virtue, all the virtue I know any thing about bids me stab the tyrant. He shall die."

"Nay, as you say that you understand me not, you may well leave to speak of what dwells without the circle of your intelligence. Are you not a priest? a man of peace? and dare you avow such thoughts? They shame your profession; and, if any spark of virtue dwelt within you, you would now blush as deep a red, as your hands would shew, stained with that blood you think to shed."

"Madonna," said Ugo, "you are now animated beyond all prudence. Speak mildly; and Messer Tripalda will yield."

"That will I not!" cried Tripalda, compressing his thin lips, and elevating his high brows. "I have doomed him to death; and he shall die. By my soul's salvation, he shall!"

"Then is your soul lost; for he shall live."

The gentle modulation of Euthanasia's voice, now first attuned to command, carried with it an irresistible force, while she extended her fair arm in earnest gesture; then, calming herself, she continued: "I entered into this conspiracy on one condition; and I might well say, 'If you keep not your words with me, neither will I keep mine with you; if you betray me, so will I betray you.' But I say not this; I have other means of silencing this man. I know you, Tripalda; and you are well aware, that I can see through the many folds which you have wound round your heart. You oblige me to menace you. I can tell a tale, Tripalda, a tale the knowledge of whose exceeding horror is confined to your own polluted heart; but whose slightest sketch would fill mankind with detestation, and your destruction would quickly follow. Dare not even to imagine the death of Castruccio; while he is safe, you are safe; otherwise you know what will follow."

"So far from knowing, I cannot even guess your meaning," replied Tripalda; but with a subdued voice and a humble manner. "In truth, Madonna, you speak enigmas to me. But since you are resolved to save the life of the prince, so let it be. But I suppose you will allow us to secure his person."

"We have a plan for that," said Euthanasia, turning to Ugo, "a plan to which I hope you will accede: for Castruccio must be saved; Bondelmonti entered into that engagement with me, before I became a party to your plot."

"It shall be as you command," replied Tripalda, who had shifted his place several times, and seemed to stand as uneasily before the now softened looks of Euthanasia, as a hypocrite well might before the eyes of the accusing angel. "I will leave you now," continued he, "for I promised to be with Nicola dei Avogadii at eight o'clock, and seven struck some time ago. Good night, Madonna; when we again meet, I hope you will be better pleased with my intentions, and thank me for my exertions in favour of your friend, the prince."

He quitted the room. Euthanasia followed him with her eyes until he had closed the door; and then she said to Ugo, "I distrust that man; and if my purpose did not lift me alike above fear and hope, I should dread him. But do you have a care, Ugo; and, if you regard your own safety, watch him, as you would one whose sword you must parry, until the deed you meditate be accomplished."

"You judge hastily, Madonna; he is the sworn enemy of Castruccio; and I believe him to be, on this occasion at least, trust-worthy. I cannot divine what you know concerning him; it is surely something black, for he cowered beneath your words. But a man may be one day wicked, and good the next; for self-interest sways all, and we are virtuous or vicious as we hope for advantage to ourselves. The downfal of Antelminelli will raise him; and therefore he is to be trusted."

"That is bad philosophy, and worse morality, Ugo: but we have no time to dispute now; remember, that I tell you to beware of Tripalda. Now let us occupy ourselves in worthier considerations."

After a long conversation, in which all was concluded except the exact period for the breaking out of the conspiracy, Ugo retired, to prepare messengers for Pisa and Florence, that they might, with the concurrence of their associates, determine the conduct of this last act of the tragedy. Euthanasia was left alone. She had been roused to the expression of anger by the insolent cruelty of Tripalda; but her nature, mild as it was, quickly forgot the feeling of indignation, and now other thoughts (oh, far other thoughts!) possessed her. She was again in Lucca. She ascended to the tower of her palace; and the waning moon, which shone in the east, shed its yellow and melancholy light over the landscape: she could distinguish afar the abrupt and isolated rock on which the castle of Valperga had stood; it formed one of the sides of the chasm which the spirits of creation had opened to make free the course of the Serchio. The scene was unchanged; and even in winter the soul of beauty hovered over it, ready again to reanimate the corpse, when the caducean wand of spring should touch it. The narrow, deep streets of Lucca lay like the allies of a prison around her; and she longed for the consummation of the deed in which she had engaged, when she might fly for ever from a scene, which had been too dear to her, not to make its sight painful in her altered situation.

In the mean time, while in deep security of thought she brooded over the success of her attempt, the hour which yet lingered on the dial was big with her ruin; and events which threatened to destroy her for ever, already came so near, that their awful shadow began to be thrown on the path of her life.

Tripalda had left her, burning with all the malice of which his evil nature was so amply susceptible. He had learned that the prisoner of the castle in the Campagna di Roma had survived, and had fallen into the hands of Euthanasia: and he knew that his fate depended upon disclosures that she was enabled to make. The prisoner was now dead; but both Castruccio and Euthanasia had become in part the depositaries of her secret; Euthanasia had heard his name pronounced, mingled with shrieks and despair, by the lips of the lovely maniac; and, after her death, she had revealed her suspicions to the prince, while he in anger forbade the priest ever again to approach his palace or his person. In disgracing and banishing him from his presence, Castruccio had incurred the penalty of his hate; and he was overjoyed to think, that in destroying the man who had injured him, he should also free himself from one who was conscious of the most perilous secrets concerning him. He had been loud in his abuse of the prince; but none had listened to him, except those who sympathized in his feelings; and Antelminelli despised him too heartily to take heed to what he said.

Thus, with the wily heart and wicked design of a serpent beneath a magpie's exterior, this self-named Brutus of modern Italy, whose feigned folly was a cover for pride, selfishness and all uncharitableness, fomented a conspiracy in Lucca to overthrow a tyrant, who well deserved to fall, but who was as pure as the milk-white dove, if compared with the sable plumage of this crow. He had endeavoured to intice Euthanasia to participate in the plot, he hardly knew why, secure that, if she were persuaded to enter into it, it would be pregnant with nothing but misery and suffering for her. The scene which had taken place in her palace, overturned all his ideas. Castruccio despised and banished him; but he had never menaced the disclosure of those secrets, whose smallest effect would be to immure him for ever within the dungeons of some convent. He therefore hated, rather than feared him; but the words of Euthanasia had terrified his soul, and with his terror awakened all those feelings of hellish malignity with which his heart was imbued. To destroy her, and save himself, was now the scope of his desire. To betray the conspiracy, and deliver over his confederates to death, was of little moment in his eyes, compared with the care he had for his own preservation, and the satisfaction of his new-born revenge. All night he slept not; he walked up and down his room, easing his heart with curses, and with images of impending ruin for his enemies. When morning dawned, he hasted to Agosta, and made his way into the private cabinet of Vanni Mordecastelli.

Castruccio was at Pistoia, and would not return until the following day; in the mean time Mordecastelli was the governor of Lucca. He was seated in his cabinet with his secretary when Tripalda entered: like a true courtier, he hardly deigned to look on the man who was disgraced by his prince.

"Messer Tripalda," said he, "are you still in Lucca? I thought some one told me that you had returned to your canonicate. Have you any business with me? Be brief; for you see that I am occupied."

"Messer Vanni, I have business with you; but it must be private. Do not look thus contemptuously on me; for you know that I have been useful to you before; and I shall now be so again."

"I do not much care to trust myself alone with you; for they say that you have sworn destruction to all the prince's friends. However, I am armed," he continued, taking a dagger from his bosom, and drawing it from it's sheath; "so, Ubaldo, you may leave us alone."

"And, Ubaldo, do you hear," cried Tripalda, "it is as much as your life is worth to tell any one that I am with the governor. The very walls of the palace must not know it."

"And are you the lord to threaten me, Messer Canonico? though you have a fool's head, pray keep a discreet tongue."

"Silence, Ubaldo," said Mordecastelli. "Go, and remember what he says: you shall answer for it, if it be known that this visit has taken place.— — And now, Sir Priest, what have you to say to me? if it be not something well worth the hearing, you shall pay a rich penalty for this impertinence of yours."

"Remember, Messer Vanni, who put you on the right scent in Leodino's plot; remember the golden harvest which that brought you in. Remember this; and put aside your pride and insolence."

"I remember well the detestable part that you then played, and it had been well that your head had been struck off instead of Leodino's. But you trifle now, and I have no time to waste; if you have any fresh scene of villainy to disclose, be quick."

"I have discovered a plot of the highest consequence. One that counts among the conspirators the first citizens of the principality. But I must make my conditions before I tell you further: I hold the life of your lord in my grasp; and, before I part with my advantage, I must be paid its full worth."

"Conditions! Aye, they shall be generous and ample ones; if you fairly tell all, you shall be believed on your word, and not be put to the torture, to extort that which craft may make you conceal: these are all the conditions a villain, such as you, deserves. Come, waste no more time; if your plot be worth the telling, you well know that you will not go unrewarded; if this is all smoke, why perchance you may be smothered in it; so no more delay."

Tripalda opened each door, peeped behind the hangings, under the tables, and chairs; and then, approaching as softly as a cat who sees a mouse playing in the moonshine, or a spider who beholds his prey unconsciously cleaning his wings within an inch of him, he sat down beside Mordecastelli and whispered:

"The Avogadii."

"Well, what of them? I know that they hate Antelminelli; but they are not powerful enough to do any mischief."

"The Quartezzani."

"Nay, then this is of deeper interest. Have they turned vipers? By St. Martin! they have a sting!"

Tripalda in a low and solemn voice entered into a detail of the plot. "And now," said he, when he had nearly concluded, "except for one circumstance, you had not heard a word of this from me."

"You are a villain to say so;—but what is this circumstance? the love you bear your prince?"

"The love I bear him might have made me bring the Pope to Lucca with thirty thousand Gascons at his heels, but not betray a plot against him. No truly it was not that; but they have admitted a woman into it; and, as there is neither safety nor success where they are, I made my retreat in good time."

"A woman! What, Berta Avogadii?"

"One of far higher rank; the countess of Valperga."

"Nay, then, it is all a lie, Tripalda, and, by the Virgin, you shall repent having amused me with your inventions! The countess of Valperga! She is too wise and too holy to mingle in one of your midnight plots: besides, once upon a time, to my knowledge she loved Castruccio."

"The old proverb tells us, Vanni, that sweetest love turns to bitterest hate. Remember Valperga! Do you think she has forgotten it? Remember her castle, her power, the state she used to keep, when she was queen of those barren mountains! Do you think she has forgotten that? She might carry it humbly; but she, like the rest of those painted ruins, is proud at heart, proud and revengeful; why she has vowed the death of her quondam lover."

"I would not believe it, if an angel were to tell me; do you think then that I will credit such a tale, when it is given out by a devil like you? Nay, do not frown, Sir Priest; the devil loves to clothe himself in a holy garb; and report says that you have more than once shewn the cloven foot."

"You are pleased to jest, Lord Governor," replied Tripalda, with a ghastly smile, "do you know the hand-writing of Orlando Quartezzani?"

"As I know my own."

"Read then that letter."

It was a letter from Orlando to Tripalda, conjuring him to be speedy in his operations, and saying that, since the countess of Valperga appeared to enter into the plot with a willing heart, all difficulties would now be easily removed.

Vanni put down the letter with a look of mingled contempt and indignation. "And who else have ye among you? I expect next to hear that some of the saints or martyrs, or perhaps the Virgin herself has come down to aid you."

"Here is a list of the conspirators; and here are letters which will serve as further proofs of the truth of my disclosures."

"Give them to me. And now let me tell you, my excellent fox, that I by no means trust you, and that, knowing your tricks of old, I may well suspect that, after trying to get all you can from us by betraying your associates, you will endeavour to get all you can out of them by assisting them to escape; so, my good fellow, you must for the present remain under lock and key."

"I hoped that I had deserved better— —"

"Deserved! Aye, you deserve the torture, as much as the vilest heretic who denies the passion of our Redeemer. You know yourself to be an arch-traitor, and, by the saints! you shall be treated like one. Come, there is a better room for your prison than you deserve: go in peaceably; for if you oblige me to use force, you shall lodge for the next week in one of those holes underground, of which I believe you have some knowledge, since your fiendish malice contrived them."

"Well, Vanni, I yield. But I hope that your future gratitude— —"

"Oh! trust to my gratitude. I know my trade too well not to encourage such hell-hounds as you are."

[4] The Dumb Knight by Machin: Act IV.

CHAPTER XI

Having thus disposed of Tripalda, Vanni sat down to study the list of conspirators that he had given him. It contained three hundred names. "What a murderous dog this priest is!" he cried. "Why every noble family has one or more of its members engaged in this plot. I shall take the liberty to curtail it exceedingly, before it meets the eyes of the prince. The ringleaders are enough for him: the rest I shall punish on my private account; a few fines will bring them to reason, and they are better subjects ever after. But Valperga! I would as soon have believed that an ass could drink up the moon, as that that villain could have drawn her from her illustrious sphere, to be swallowed up among the rest of the gulls, when he wants to make merry with a few murders. But, by St. Martin! as she has sown, so must she reap; and I hate her ten times the more for her hypocritical, angel face. Conspire against Castruccio! He used her ill; but a meek and forbearing woman's love that forgave all injuries, is what she ever boasted, if not in words, at least in looks and manners. For thy sake, thou goodly painted saint, like the rest of them, well looking outside, but worms and corruption within, I will never trust more to any of thy sex!—Nor shalt thou escape. Others will pay a fearful penalty for their treason; and thine, which merits much more than theirs, shall not go free. I could have staked my life upon Euthanasia; I knew her from a child; I remember her a smiling cherub with deep blue eyes and curly tresses; and her very name seemed to carry a divinity with it. I have many sins on my head; and, when my death comes, many years of purgatory may be tacked on to my absolution; but methought that, when I contemplated and almost adored the virtues of Euthanasia, my soul was half-way through its purification;—and she to fall!"

Vanni, who, in the common acceptation, was truly faithful to his master, was struck with disgust at what appeared to him the depth of treachery on her part. He knew little of the human heart, its wondrous subtlety and lawyer-like distinctions; he could not imagine the thousand sophistries that cloaked her purpose to Euthanasia, the veils of woven wind, that made her apparent treachery shew like purest truth to her. He could not judge of the enthusiasm, that, although it permitted her to foresee the opprobrium and condemnation which would be attached to her conduct, yet made her trample upon all. She walked on in what she deemed the right path; and neither the pangs of doubt, nor the imminent risque that awaited her perseverance, could arrest her; or, worse than all, the harsh opinion of man, his ever ready censure of ideas he cannot understand, his fiery scorn of virtue which he might never attain. She passed on to her goal, fearless of, and despising "the barbed tongues, or thoughts more sharp than they," which threatened to wound her most sacred feelings.

But Vanni could not penetrate the inner sanctuary of her heart, which throned self-approbation as its deity, and cared not for the false gods that usurp the pleasant groves and high places of the world. After having vented his spleen with that sceptred infallibility men assume, and condemned her and her whole sex unheard, Mordecastelli proceeded to more active business, and before night the chiefs of the conspiracy were thrown into prison.

Early the following morning Castruccio returned to Lucca. Mordecastelli met him with a countenance, in which the falcon-eye of the prince could read uncommon tidings. "Why do you look thus, my friend?" said he. "Either laugh or cry; or tell me why you do neither, although on the verge of both."

"My lord, I have cause. I have discovered a conspiracy which threatened your power, and that not a mean one; so that I must wish you joy, that you have again escaped from these harpies. But, when you hear the names of the conspirators, you also will be sorrowful; several of your friends are among them; and names, which have been repeated in your daily prayers with blessings joined to them, are now written in the list of traitors."

"When I took power upon me, my dear Vanni, I well knew that I wrapt suspicion about me as a robe, and wedded danger, and treachery, and most other evils. So let it be! I was yet a boy, when I prayed to be a prince, though my crown were of thorns. But who are these? Which of my old friends are so blind, as to see their own interest in my downfal?"

Mordecastelli gave the list of the ringleaders which he had prepared, and watched the countenance of Castruccio as he read it. He observed contempt and carelessness on his countenance, until the name of the countess of Valperga met his eyes; he then saw the expression change, and a slight convulsion on his lips, which he evidently strove to suppress. Vanni could contain himself no longer.

"You see, my lord, you see her name. And, as true as there is a sun in heaven, as true, as she is false, this saintlike Euthanasia has spotted her soul with treason. I have proofs, here they are. It would make one doubt one's salvation, to see her with her Madona face creep into this nest of traitors. There they must have been, closeted in a cellar, or hid in some dark hole; for else my spies would have earthed them out long ago. And I figure her to myself, with her golden hair, and eyes which illumined even the night, they were so dazzling,—entering a room made dark enough to hide treason;— and to think that the hellish bat did not take wing out at the window when she appeared! but no, she cherished him in her bosom."

"You are eloquent, Vanni."

"I am, my lord. I took her for an angel, and I find her a woman;—one of those frail, foolish creatures we all despise——"

"Peace, peace, my dear Vanni; you talk insufferable nonsense. Let us proceed to more serious business. What have you done with these people?"

"They are all in prison."

"The countess among them?"

"Why, my lord, would you have had her spared?"

"She is in prison then?"

"She is."

"Vanni, you must look to these people. I assure you that I by no means find myself mercifully inclined towards them. These continual plots, and this foolish ingratitude, to give it no worse name, disturb our government too much. I will tear it away root and branch; and the punishment of these fellows shall be a terrible warning to those who may think of treading in the same steps."

Castruccio fixed his eyes upon Mordecastelli; but there was an expression in them that made the confident cast his upon the ground. They glared; and his pale face became paler, so that his very lips were white. He looked steadily on Mordecastelli for some minutes; and then said:

"They must all die."

"They shall, my lord."

"Yet not by an easy death. That were a poor revenge. They shall die, as they have lived, like traitors; and on their living tombs shall be written, Thus Castruccio punishes his rebel subjects. Have I toiled, exposed my person to danger, become the fear and hope of Tuscany, to stain with my best blood the dagger of one of these miserable villains? Do you see that they die so, Vanni, as that I may be satisfied."

"I will, my lord. And the countess?" —

"Leave her to me. I will be her judge and executioner."

"Castruccio?"

"Do not look so pale, Vanni; you do not understand. A few hours hence I will tell you more. Now leave me."

Solitude is a coy companion for a prince, and one he little loves. But Castruccio had much to occupy his thoughts, much that agonized him. "Revenge!" He clenched his hand, and, throwing his eyes upward, he cried: "Yes, revenge is among those few goods in life, which compensate for its many evils. Yet it is poor: it is a passion which can have no end. Burning in pursuit, cold and unsatisfactory in its conclusion, it is as love, which wears out its soul in unrequited caresses. But still, it shall be mine; and these shall suffer. They shall feel in every nerve what it is to have awakened me. I will not fear; I will not feel my life depend alone upon the word of these most impotent slaves. They shall die; and the whole world shall learn that Castruccio can revenge."

Thus he thought: yet there was an inner sense, that betrayed to him the paltriness of his feelings, when he imagined that there was glory in trampling upon the enemy beneath his feet. He would not listen to this small still voice; but, turning from these ideas, he began to reflect on that which filled him with a bitterness of feeling to which he had long been a stranger.

"So, she has conspired against me; and, forgetful of all those ties that bound us notwithstanding her coldness, she has plotted my death! She knew, she must have known, that in spite of absence and repulse, she was the saint of my life; and that this one human weakness, or human virtue, remained to me, when power and a strong will had in other respects metamorphosed me. Does she forget, that I have ever worn near my heart a medallion engraven with her vows of childhood? She has forgotten all. And not only has she forgotten to love, but she, has cast aside the uprightness of her understanding, and stained the purity of her soul.

"It is well for me to speak thus, who, instead of the virtues that once were mine, have as ministers, revenge, and hate, and conquest. But, although I choose to be thus, and although I have selected these hell-hounds to drag my car of life, I have not lost the sense of what is just and right; and, in the midst of all my wilful errors and my degradation, I could discern and worship the pure loveliness of Euthanasia. By the saints! I believed, that, if she died, like Dante's Beatrice, she would plead for me before the throne of the Eternal, and that I should be saved through her. Now she is lost, and may perdition seize the whole worthless race of man, since it has fallen upon her!

"But SHE MUST BE SAVED. My hands shall not be stained with her blood, nor my soul bear the brand of that crime. But she must not stay here; nor shall she remain in Tuscany. She shall go far away, so that I never more may hear her name: that shall be her punishment, and she must bear it. Now I must contrive the means; for she shall not remain another night in prison."

Euthanasia in prison! Yes; she had become the inhabitant of this abode of crime, though her high mind was as far above fault as human nature could soar; hers, if it were an error, was one of judgement. But why should I call it error? To remove a cruel tyrant from his seat of power,—to devote those days, which she might have spent in luxury and pleasure, to a deep solitude, where neither love nor sympathy would cheer her;—to bear his anger, perhaps his hate, and in the midst of all to preserve a firmness and sweetness, that might sustain her, and soften him,—to quit all her friends, and her native country for ever, to follow in the steps of one she had ceased to love, but to whom she felt herself for ever bound by her wish to preserve him from that misery which his crimes would ultimately occasion him: these were her errors.

After Quartezzani had quitted her on the night of her arrival in Lucca, she had not slept; she was too full of various thought, of dread and breathless expectation, to compose her spirits to rest. She felt eternity in each second; and each slow hour seemed to creep forward, stretching itself in a wide, endless circle around her. When day dawned, it found her, not sleeping, but with open eyes looking on the one last star that faded in the west, calling to mind a thousand associations, a thousand hopes, now lying dead in the ashes of that pyre time had heaped together and consumed; she looked forward; yet then she paused; she dared not attempt to penetrate into futurity;—all was so tempestuous and dark.

She arose at sun-rise, and had descended into the garden, to breathe the bleak, but, to her feverish spirits the refreshing air of a December morning; when, at noon, Quartezzani rushed in; he was deadly pale, and his hair seemed to stand on end with fear.

"Holy saints! what has happened?" cried Euthanasia.

"We are all lost! dead, or worse than dead! We are betrayed!"

"Tripalda has betrayed us?"

"He has."

"And there is no escape?"

"None. The gates are shut, nor will they be opened, until we are all seized."

"Then most certainly we die?"

"As sure as that Christ died upon the cross! so surely shall we perish."

"Then courage, my friend, and let us cast aside, with all mortal hopes, all mortal fear. I have the start of you, Ugo; I was prepared for this; but you would not believe me, until now my predictions are sealed by the event.

Let us die, as we would have lived, for the cause of freedom; and let no trembling dismay, no coward fear, make us the mock of our enemies.

"Other men in various ages have died by untimely death, and we will dare to imitate them. Others have sustained their fate with fortitude; and let faith and submission to the will of heaven be to us, instead of that dauntless spirit of inbred virtue that supported the heroes of antiquity."

Euthanasia raised her own spirits as she spoke; and fearless expectation, and something like triumph, illuminated her countenance, as she cast her eyes upward, and with her hand clasped that of her friend. He received no warmth from the pressure; chilly fear possessed him; and he stood utterly dejected before her—he wept.

"Aye, weep," she continued, "and I also, did not the tempest of my soul bear all clouds far away, I also might shed tears. You weep to leave those whom you love, ——that is a bitter pang. You weep to see your associates suffer; but each must relieve the other from that sorrow by cheerfulness and courage. But," she continued, seeing him entirely subdued by fear, "is there no hope of escape? Exert your ingenuity; once past the gates, you would soon be out of the territory of Lucca. And Castruccio——"

"Oh, that most hated name! Bloody, execrable tyrant! Curse him! May the fiends——"

"Cease! know you not that a dying man's curse falls more on himself, than on him against whom he imprecates the wrath of heaven? This is childish; Ugo, collect yourself; you have a wife;—woman's wit is ready; consult with her; she may devise some plan for your safety."

"You are an angel of consolation, Euthanasia. Heaven bless you! and do you also reflect on your own danger."

He left her: and she (without giving a thought to vain regret; her moments were too precious) sat down and wrote a long letter to Bondelmonti. It was calm and affectionate: she felt raised above mortality; and her words expressed the exceeding serenity of her soul. She gave a last farewel to her friends. "It may seem strange to you," she wrote, "that I express myself thus: and indeed, when I reason with myself, methinks I ought not to expect death from the hands of Antelminelli. Nor do I; and yet I expect some solemn termination to this scene, some catastrophe which will divide me from you for ever. Nor is it Italy, beloved and native Italy, that I shall leave, but also this air, this sun, and the earth's beauty. I feel thus; and therefore do I write you an eternal farewel."

She had scarcely finished her letter, when a messenger arrived from Mordecastelli. He told her that the conspiracy was divulged, and that she must in a prison await the orders of Castruccio. She started at the word *Prison*; but, recovering herself, she made a sign that she was ready to follow the messenger; so, without a word, without a sigh, she quitted her palace, and, ascending her litter, was conducted to her place of confinement. She passed through the same streets, through which the jailor had conducted her to the dungeon of Beatrice. A small and curiously carved shrine of the Madona with a lamp before it, chanced to recal this circumstance to her mind. "Thou art at peace, blessed one," she said, "there where I hope soon to be."

The jailor of the prison, who was the same that had besought her to come and comfort poor Beatrice, received her with a sorrowful countenance, and led her to his most decent apartment, high in the tower, that overlooked the rest of the building. There she was left alone to ruminate on her fortunes, and to imbue herself with that fortitude, which might carry her with honour through the trials that awaited her. The circumstance that pressed most painfully upon her, was the death which her associates must suffer. She tried to forget herself; she did not fear death; she did not expect it at the hands of Castruccio; and her expectations and ideas were too vague to permit her to dread much the coming events as they regarded her. The window of her prison-chamber was not grated, and from it she could survey the neighbouring country. A thousand feelings passed through her mind, and she could put no order in her thoughts. Sleep refused to visit her; but her reflections became peaceful, and full of pleasant images and recollections.

Morning succeeded to a winter's night. It was clear, and sunshiny, but cold. The cheering beams poured into her room; she looked upon the azure sky, and the flock of giant mountains which lay crouching around, with a strange pleasure. She felt as if she saw them for the last time, but as if she were capable of enjoying until the latest moment those pleasures which nature had ever conferred upon her. She repeated some of Dante's verses where he describes in such divine strains the solemn calm and celestial beauty of paradise. "When will it be my lot to wander there also," she said, "when shall I enjoy the windless air, and flower-starred meadows of that land?"

Thus the whole day passed; but it was quickly dark; and she, who had watched for two nights, and was now quite overcome, looking out once upon the evening star, that star she had ever loved, and which was ever to her as the good genius of the world watching his children in their repose, repeated the Catholic ejaculation, "*Stella, alma, benigna, ora pro nobis!*" then, crossing herself, she lay down to rest, and quickly slept, as peacefully and happily, as a babe rocked in its mother's arms.

CHAPTER XII

A little before midnight Euthanasia's prison-chamber was unlocked, and the jailor entered, with a lamp in his hand, accompanied by one of majestic figure, and a countenance beautiful, but sad, and tarnished by the expression of pride that animated it. "She sleeps," whispered the jailor. His companion raised his finger in token of silence; and, taking the lamp from the man's hand, approached her mattress which was spread upon the floor, and, kneeling down beside it, earnestly gazed upon that face he had known so well in happier days. She made an uneasy motion, as if the lamp which he held disturbed her; he placed it on the ground, and shaded it with his figure; while, by the soft light that fell upon her, he tried to read the images that were working in her mind.

She appeared but slightly altered since he had first seen her. If thought had drawn some lines in her brow, the intellect which its beautiful form expressed, effaced them to the eye of the spectator: her golden hair fell over her face and neck: he gently drew it back, while she smiled in her sleep; her smile was ever past description lovely, and one might well exclaim with Dante

> Quel, ch' ella par quando un poco sorride,
> Non si puo dicer, ne tenere a mente;
> Si è nuovo miracolo, e gentile [5] .

He gazed on her long; her white arm lay on her black dress, and he imprinted a sad kiss upon it; she awoke, and saw Castruccio gazing upon her.

She started up; "What does this mean?" she cried.

His countenance, which had softened as he looked upon her, now reassumed its severe expression. "Madonna," he replied, "I come to take you from this place."

She looked on him, endeavouring to read his purpose in his eyes; but she saw there no explanation of her doubts:—"And whither do you intend to lead me?"

"That you will know hereafter."

She paused; and he added with a disdainful smile, "The countess of Valperga need not fear, while I have the power to protect her, the fate she prepared for me."

"What fate?"

"Death."

He spoke in an under tone, but with one of those modulations of voice, which, bringing to her mind scenes of other days, was best fitted to make an impression upon her. She replied almost unconsciously—"I did not prepare death for you; God is my witness!"

"Well, Madonna, we will not quarrel about words; or, like lawyers, clothe our purposes in such a subtle guise, that it might deceive all, if truth did not destroy the spider's web. I come to lead you from prison."

"Not thus, my lord, not thus will I be saved. I disdain any longer to assert my intentions, since I am not believed. But am I to be liberated alone; or are my friends included in your merciful intentions?"

"Your friends are too dangerous enemies of the commonwealth, to be rescued from the fate that awaits them. Your sex, perhaps the memory of our ancient friendship, plead for you; and I do not think that it accords with your wisdom to make conditions with one who has the power to do that which best pleases him."

"And yet I will not yield; I will not most unworthily attend to my own safety, while my associates die. No, my lord, if they are to be sacrificed, the addition of one poor woman will add little to the number of your victims; and I cannot consent to desert them."

"How do you desert them? You will never see or hear of them more, or they of you. But this is trifling; and my moments are precious."

"I will not—I dare not follow you. My heart, my conscience tell me to remain. I must not disobey their voice."

"Is your conscience so officious now, and did it say nothing, or did your heart silence it, when you plotted my destruction?"

"Castruccio, this I believe is the last time that I shall ever speak to you. Our hearts are in the hands of the father of all; and he sees my thoughts. You know me too well, to believe that I plotted your death, or that of any human creature. Now is not the time to explain my motives and plans: but my earnest prayer was that you might live; my best hope, to make that life less miserable, less unworthy, than it had hitherto been."

She spoke with deep earnestness; and there was something in her manner, as if the spirit of truth animated all her accents, that compelled assent. Castruccio believed all; and he spoke in a milder and more persuasive manner "Poor Euthanasia! so you were at last cajoled by that arch-traitor, Bondelmonti. Well, I believe, and pardon all; but, as the seal of the purity of your intentions, I now claim your consent to my offers of safety."

"I cannot, indeed I cannot, consent. Be merciful; be magnanimous; and pardon all, banish us all where our discontent cannot be dangerous to you. But to desert my friends, and basely to save that life you deny to them, I never can."

The jailor, who had hitherto stood in the shade near the door, could no longer contain himself. He knelt to Euthanasia, and earnestly and warmly intreated her to save herself, and not with wilful presumption to cast aside those means which God had brought about for her safety. "Remember," he cried, "your misfortunes will be on the prince's head; make him not answer for you also. Oh! lady, for his sake, for all our sakes, yield."

Castruccio was much moved to see the warmth of this man. He took the hand of Euthanasia, he also knelt: "Yes, my only and dearest friend, save yourself for my sake. Yield, beloved Euthanasia, to my intreaties. Indeed you will not die; for you well know that your life is dearer to me than my own. But yield to my request, by our former loves, I intreat; by the prayers which you offer up for my salvation, I conjure you as they shall be heard, so also hear me!"

The light of the solitary lamp fell full upon the countenance of Castruccio: it was softened from all severity; his eyes glistened, and a tear stole silently down his cheek as he prayed her to yield. They talk of the tears of women; but, when they flow most plenteously, they soften not the heart of man, as one tear from his eyes has power on a woman. Words and looks have been feigned; they say, though I believe them not, that women have feigned tears: but those of a man, which are ever as the last demonstration of a too full heart, force belief, and communicate to her who causes them, that excess of tenderness, that intense depth of passion, of which they are themselves the sure indication.

Euthanasia had seen Castruccio weep but once before; it was many years ago, when he departed for the battle of Monte Catini; and he then sympathized too deeply in her sorrows, not to repay her much weeping with one most true and sacred tear. And now this scene was present before her; the gap of years remained unfilled; and she had consented to his request, before she again recalled her thoughts, and saw the dreary prison-chamber, the glimmering lamp, and the rough form of the jailor who knelt beside

Antelminelli. Her consent was scarcely obtained, when Castruccio leapt up, and, bidding her wrap her capuchin about her, led her by the hand down the steep prison-stairs, while the jailor went before them, and unlocked, and drew back the bolts of, the heavy, creaking doors.

At the entrance of the prison they found a man on horseback holding two other horses. It was Mordecastelli. Castruccio assisted Euthanasia to mount, and then sprang on his own saddle; they walked their horses to a gate of the town which was open;—they proceeded in silence;—at the gate Castruccio said to his companion—"Here leave us; I shall speedily return."

Vanni then turned his horse's head, slightly answering the salute of Euthanasia, which she had involuntarily made at parting for ever with one who had been her intimate acquaintance. A countryman was waiting on horseback outside the gate: "You are our guide?" said Castruccio. "Lead on then."

It was a frosty, cloudless night; there was no moon, but the stars shone intensely above; the bright assemblage seemed to congregate from the far wastes of heaven, and to press in innumerable clusters upon the edge of the visible atmosphere, to gaze upon the strange earth beneath. The party passed out of the city of Lucca by the Pisan gate, and at first put their horses to a gallop. As they approached the hills, Castruccio came up beside Euthanasia; they slackened their speed; she spoke thus:

"I have acceded to your request, and left the prison; indeed it were useless in me to resist one who possesses the absolute power that you do. But I intreat you now that I see you for the last time, to have pity on my companions in this conspiracy. I can think only of them; and if I am to live— if ever I am again to hear of the events which will pass within the walls of that town, reflect on the sharp pang you will inflict upon me, if I hear of their destruction."

"Madonna," replied the prince, "I will do that which I consider my duty: and let not these our last moments be employed in fruitless discussion."

Euthanasia felt that it was in vain to speak. Her confederates, her friends, who were reserved instantly to die, stood in funereal groupe before the eye of her soul; her imagination made present to her all that they thought, and all that they were to suffer. She looked upon Castruccio; she saw that he was moulded of an impenetrable substance: her heart swelled to the confines of her bosom, and forbade her such degradation to the assured victims, as would be implied in her uttering one further word in their behalf to the unhearing, unrelenting being that stood before her. Castruccio continued:

"You are about to leave Tuscany, and to take up your abode in a foreign land. You are still young. I send you from your native country; but you may at a future period confess that I have done you a kindness. You have hitherto mingled in the embroiled politics of a republic, and seen conspiracies, heart-burnings, and war."

Euthanasia felt herself unable to reply.

They had crossed the plain of Lucca, and were arrived beneath those hills, which, crowned with towers, and clothed with deep forests, were the beautiful romantic steeps that she best loved. They struck off here from the usual road, and, fording the Serchio, began to ascend the acclivities on the opposite side, proceeding one by one up the narrow path. At length they reached the summit, and viewed, stretched before them beneath the stars of night, a scene of enchanting beauty. The plain they had just crossed was dimly seen beneath, bounded by its hills; before them was another plain, desert and barren, through which the Serchio flows, bounded by the dark line of the sea; and the Lago di Macciucoli, a marshy lake, was close beneath.

"Here I leave you," said Castruccio: "there is your destination," and he pointed to the sea; "remember one with whom you have passed your happiest days."

He took her hand, and kissed it. Her feelings were strange, and hardly to be described. She could not entirely forget what he had once been to her. She could at that moment have overlooked his tyranny, his lawless ambition, and his cruelty. But, no; the moment itself was a bane to oblivion. She could have forgotten his past cruelties, but not those which were immediately to be perpetrated, to be perpetrated on individuals who had been united with her in a plot for liberty, and some of whom her name and her countenance had perhaps prompted to the desperate undertaking, and egged on to destruction.

Castruccio spoke to the guide, recommending haste as soon as they should reach the plain, and then turned his horse's head. Euthanasia and her conductor paused on the summit of the hill; and she heard the steps of Castruccio's horse, as it made its way back through the tangled underwood. Then she also began her descent on the other side.

Euthanasia, being now separated from her former connections, and from him who had been the evil genius of the scene, began to resume her wonted tone. The eternal spirit of the universe seemed to descend upon her, and she drank in breathlessly the sensation, which the silent night, the starry heavens, and the sleeping earth bestowed upon her. All seemed so peaceful, that no unwelcome sensation in her own heart could disturb the scene of which she felt herself a part. She looked up, and exclaimed in her own beautiful Italian, whose soft accents and expressive phrases then so much transcended all other European languages—"What a brave canopy has this earth, and how graciously does the supreme empyrean smile upon its nursling!"

"*E Bellissimo,*" replied her guide, "*ma figuratevi, Madonna, se è tanto bello sul rovescio, cosa mai sarà al dritto* [6]."

Euthanasia smiled at the fancy of one so uncouth in manners and habits of life; and she replied,—"Who knows how soon it may be my destiny to see that other side, which you imagine outdoes this sublime spectacle in splendour?"

"Heaven preserve you long upon earth," replied the man; "and make you as happy as you deserve, as happy as you have made others!"

"Do you know me then?"

"I dwell in the village of Valperga. I and my family have been Aldiani there, since the time of the old count Goffredo, your great-grandfather. But, Madonna, please you to put spur to your horse; for we have little time, and I fear that before long the heavens will be overclouded; that last puff had something of the scirocco in it, and I see a mist in the west that foretels wind from that quarter."

They put their horses to the gallop. Euthanasia's was a noble steed, and bore her proudly on. She felt her spirits rise with the exhilarating motion; the wind gathered from the west, and scattered her hair, which, as she quitted her prison, she had slightly bound with a handkerchief; and, as she faced the breeze, its warm breath brought the lagging blood to her cheeks.

They approached the sea, and began to hear its roar; the breeze became stronger as they drew near. The beach was flat, and the small line of sand that bordered the waters, was now beaten upon, and covered by the waves. As they came near, Euthanasia felt some curiosity to know her destination; but she saw nothing but the dim weed-grown field, and the white breakers of the troubled ocean. It was not until they were close upon the sand, that she discerned a large black boat drawn up on the beach, and several men near it. One of them came up, and asked the word, which the countryman gave; and then a man, who had the appearance of a leader, came from the boat, and welcomed Euthanasia.—"I am commanded," he said, "by the prince of Lucca to receive you, lady."

"And whither am I to go?"

He pointed to a vessel which rode hard by,—so near, that she wondered she had not seen it before. Its black hulk cast a deep shade upon the waters;

and the dim sails, increased to an extraordinary size by the darkness, flapped heavily. She looked upon it with surprize, and wondered whither it was to bear her; but she asked no more questions: addressing herself for her departure, she took a kind leave of the countryman, and gave him the little gold that she had with her. The man turned to the chief, and said,—"Sir knight, if it be not thought impertinent, have the courtesy to inform me whither that vessel is bound."

The man looked at him somewhat haughtily: but replied—"To Sicily." Sicily was then under the rule of the family of the kings of Arragon, who inherited from the daughter of Manfred, and were of course Ghibelines.

"The Virgin Mother bless your voyage!" said her guide to Euthanasia.— "I am afraid that it will be rough, for an ugly wind is rising: but the saints will surely guard you."

Euthanasia stepped into the boat; its commander sat beside her; and the men took their oars: she waved her hand to her guide, saying, "Farewel, may God bless you!" she added in a low tone, half to herself—"They speak Italian also in Sicily."

These were the last words she ever spoke to any one who returned to tell the tale. The countryman stood upon the beach;—he saw the boat moor beside the vessel; he saw its crew ascend the dark sides. The boat was drawn up; the sails were set; and they bore out to sea, receding slowly with many tacks, for the wind was contrary;—the vessel faded on the sight; and he turned about, and speeded to Lucca.

The wind changed to a more northerly direction during the night; and the land-breeze of the morning filled their sails, so that, although slowly, they dropt down southward. About noon they met a Pisan vessel, who bade them beware of a Genoese squadron, which was cruizing off Corsica: so they bore in nearer to the shore. At sunset that day a fierce scirocco rose, accompanied by thunder and lightning, such as is seldom seen during the winter season. Presently they saw huge, dark columns, descending from heaven, and meeting the sea, which boiled beneath; they were borne on by the storm, and scattered by the wind. The rain came down in sheets; and the hail clattered, as it fell to its grave in the ocean;—the ocean was lashed into such waves, that, many miles inland, during the pauses of the wind, the hoarse and constant murmurs of the far-off sea made the well-housed landsman mutter one more prayer for those exposed to its fury.

Such was the storm, as it was seen from shore. Nothing more was ever known of the Sicilian vessel which bore Euthanasia. It never reached its destined port, nor were any of those on board ever after seen. The centinels who watched near Vado, a tower on the sea beach of the Maremma, found on the following day, that the waves had washed on shore some of the wrecks of a vessel; they picked up a few planks and a broken mast, round which, tangled with some of its cordage, was a white silk handkerchief, such a one as had bound the tresses of Euthanasia the night that she had embarked, and in its knot were a few golden hairs.

She was never heard of more; even her name perished. She slept in the oozy cavern of the ocean; the sea-weed was tangled with her shining hair; and the spirits of the deep wondered that the earth had trusted so lovely a creature to the barren bosom of the sea, which, as an evil step-mother, deceives and betrays all committed to her care.

Earth felt no change when she died; and men forgot her. Yet a lovelier spirit never ceased to breathe, nor was a lovelier form ever destroyed amidst the many it brings forth. Endless tears might well have been shed at her loss; yet for her none wept, save the piteous skies, which deplored the mischief they had themselves committed;—none moaned except the sea-birds that flapped their heavy wings above the ocean-cave wherein she lay;—and the muttering thunder alone tolled her passing bell, as she quitted a life, which for her had been replete with change and sorrow.

[5] Vita Nuova di Dante.

[6] I could not refrain from recording in their original language the words of a Florentine peasant. A poet might well envy the vivacity of this man's imagination.

CONCLUSION

The private chronicles, from which the foregoing relation has been collected, end with the death of Euthanasia. It is therefore in public histories alone that we find an account of the last years of the life of Castruccio. We can know nothing of his grief, when he found that she whom he had once tenderly loved, and whom he had ever revered as the best and wisest among his friends, had died. We know however that, during the two years that he survived this event, his glory and power arose not only higher than they had ever before done, but that they surpassed those of any former Italian prince.

Louis of Bavaria, king of the Romans, entered Italy in the month of February 1327. He found Castruccio, the scourge of the Guelphs, the first power of Tuscany, and the principal supporter of his own titles and pretensions.

Louis of Bavaria was crowned with the iron crown at Milan. But his proceedings were tyrannical and imprudent. He deprived Galeazzo Visconti of his power, imprisoned him, and set up the shadow of a republic at Milan, which was in fact composed of a few Ghibeline nobles, who by their jealousies and dissentions served only to weaken his power.

He marched through Lombardy, crossed the Apennines at Parma, and was met by Castruccio at Pontremoli. The prince, whose chief aim was to ingratiate himself with, and to raise himself to power through the favour of, the emperor, made his visit more agreeable through the magnificent presents by which he was accompanied; and his sagacity, warlike spirit, and agreeable manners gained for him an easy entrance into the councils, and afterwards into the friendship, of Louis. They proceeded together to Pisa. The Pisans at first refused entrance to the emperor, but yielded after he had besieged them a few days. Louis then visited Lucca, where he erected a dutchy composed of the towns and territory of Lucca, Pistoia, Volterra and

Lunigiana, and created Castruccio duke, honouring and exalting him as his best friend, and the firmest support of the imperial power.

They went to Rome together, where the emperor knighted him, and he bore the sword of state in the procession from the Campidoglio to St. Peter's, where Louis received the imperial crown. He was created count of the palace, senator of Rome, and master of the court. He had arrived at the summit of his glory; he was more feared and obeyed than the emperor himself; and, in the expedition which Louis meditated against Naples, king Robert dreaded Castruccio alone, as his most formidable and craftiest enemy. It was then, that the proud Antelminelli invested himself in a robe of silk richly adorned with gold and jewels; and on the breast were embroidered these words— EGLI È COME DIO VUOLE. And on the shoulders, È SI SARA QUEL CHE DIO VORRÀ.

While he was thus enjoying the maturity of his glory, and partaking all the amusements and feasts of the capital of Italy, he received intelligence that the Florentines had possessed themselves of Lucca. Without a moment's delay, he quitted Rome, traversed the Maremma with a small band of friends, and appeared, when he was least expected, in the midst of his enemies.

It was here that he again met Galeazzo Visconti. At Castruccio's request the emperor had released him from prison; and he came to serve under the ensigns of his more fortunate friend. Their meeting was an occasion of mutual joy; they embraced each other affectionately, and confirmed and renewed the vows of friendship and support which they had entered into more than ten years before. Castruccio enjoyed for a short time the unalloyed pleasure which the society of his friend afforded him; they recounted to each other their various fortunes; and, in recording the events which had passed since their separation, Galeazzo found, that, if he had lost sovereignty and power, Castruccio had lost that which might be considered far more valuable; he had lost his dearest friends; and on his pale cheek might be read, that, although he disdained to acknowledge the power of fortune, she had made him feel in his heart's core her poisoned shafts. We know nothing of the private communion of these friends; but we may guess that, if Castruccio revealed the sorrows of his heart, Galeazzo might have regretted that, instead of having instigated the ambition, and destroyed the domestic felicity of his friend, he had not taught him other lessons, through which he might have enjoyed that peace, sympathy and happiness, of which he was now for ever deprived.

His presence restored the state of his affairs. He possessed himself of Pisa, recovered Pistoia, and again returned in triumph to Lucca. But this was the term of his victories. During the siege of Pistoia he had tasked his strength beyond human suffering; he was ever in the trenches on horseback, or on foot exposed to the hot sun of July, encouraging the soldiers, directing the pioneers, and often, in the ardour of impatience, he himself took the spade, and worked among them. He neither rested nor slept; and the heats of noon-day, and the dews of night alike fell upon him. Immediately on his return to his native city, he was seized with a malignant fever. He knew that he was about to die; and, with that coolness and presence of mind which was his peculiar characteristic, he made every arrangement necessary for the welfare of Lucca, and gave particular directions to his captains for the prosecution of the war. But he felt, that he left behind him no fitting successor; and that, if he were the sole creator and only support of the Lucchese, so they would fall into their primitive insignificance when he expired. Lying thus on the bed of pain, and conscious that in a few hours he must surely die, he grasped the hand of Vanni Mordecastelli, who wept beside him, saying: *Io morrò, e vedrete il mondo per varie turbolenze confondersi, e rivoltarsi ogni cosa.* This consideration cast a gloom over his last moments; yet he supported himself with courage.

Galeazzo Visconti had assisted Castruccio in all his labours, exposing himself with like imprudence, and labouring with equal energy. He was attacked at Pistoia with the same fever and the same symptoms. Hearing that the prince was ill at Lucca, he desired, although dying, to be conveyed to him. He was carried as far as Pescia, where he expired on the third of September 1328.

On the same day, and at the same hour, Castruccio died at Lucca.

His enemies rejoiced in his death; his friends were confounded and overthrown. They, as the last act of gratitude, conducted the pomp of his funeral with princely magnificence. He was buried in the church of San Francesco, then without, now included within, the walls of Lucca. The antient tombstone is still seen on the walls of the church; and its inscription may serve for the moral and conclusion of this tale.

EN VIVO VIVAMQUE
FAMA RERUM GESTARUM
ITALICÆ MILITIÆ SPLENDOR;
LUCENSIUM
DECUS ETRURIÆ
ORNAMENTUM CASTRUCCIUS
GERII ANTELMINELLORUM
STIRPE
VIXI PECCAVI DOLUI
CESSI NATURÆ INDIGENTI
ANIMÆ PIÆ BENEVOLI
SUCCURRITE BREVI MEMORES
VOS MORITUROS.